First-da

OKAY, THERE'S

but I don't think

"I've just been

ria by Melissa Tai

Harvey licked his lips and pushed away his pizza crust. "So you might want to take a look at your fingers. And your arm."

"What?" Sophie loved Harvey, of course she did, but sometimes she feared for his sanity. "Is this another one of your nonverbal communication things? Because it's not funny."

"Soph," Kara said in a soft voice as she continued to stare. "He's not joking. You really need to look at your arm."

Sophie shot them both a look before she cautiously peered down at her arm (which, thanks to this boiling weather and her short-sleeved T-shirt, was almost fully exposed). Then she only just resisted the urge to scream as she looked at her other arm and realized her friends really hadn't been joking.

As far as she could make out, she was completely orange.

OTHER BOOKS YOU MAY ENJOY

The Books of Elsewhere, Volume 1: *The Shadows*	Jacqueline West
The Books of Elsewhere, Volume 2: *Spellbound*	Jacqueline West
Eleven	Lauren Myracle
Gilda Joyce, Psychic Investigator	Jennifer Allison
Lights, Camera, Cassidy, Episode 1: *Celebrity*	Linda Gerber
Lights, Camera, Cassidy, Episode 2: *Paparazzi*	Linda Gerber
Olivia Kidney	Ellen Potter
Sophie's Mixed-Up Magic, Book 2: *Under a Spell*	Amanda Ashby
Sophie's Mixed-Up Magic, Book 3: *Out of Sight*	Amanda Ashby
The Witchy Worries of Abbie Adams	Rhonda Hayter

Sophie's MIXED-UP Magic

Wishful Thinking

Amanda Ashby

PUFFIN BOOKS
An Imprint of Penguin Group (USA) Inc.

PUFFIN BOOKS
Published by the Penguin Group
Penguin Young Readers Group, 345 Hudson Street, New York, New York 10014, U.S.A.
Penguin Group (Canada), 90 Eglinton Avenue East, Suite 700, Toronto, Ontario, Canada M4P 2Y3
(a division of Pearson Penguin Canada Inc.)
Penguin Books Ltd, 80 Strand, London WC2R 0RL, England
Penguin Ireland, 25 St Stephen's Green, Dublin 2, Ireland (a division of Penguin Books Ltd)
Penguin Group (Australia), 250 Camberwell Road, Camberwell, Victoria 3124, Australia
(a division of Pearson Australia Group Pty Ltd)
Penguin Books India Pvt Ltd, 11 Community Centre, Panchsheel Park, New Delhi - 110 017, India
Penguin Group (NZ), 67 Apollo Drive, Rosedale, Auckland 0632, New Zealand
(a division of Pearson New Zealand Ltd)
Penguin Books (South Africa) (Pty) Ltd, 24 Sturdee Avenue,
Rosebank, Johannesburg 2196, South Africa

Penguin Books Ltd, Registered Offices: 80 Strand, London WC2R 0RL, England

Published by Puffin Books, a member of Penguin Young Readers Group, 2012

1 3 5 7 9 10 8 6 4 2

LIBRARY OF CONGRESS CATALOGING-IN-PUBLICATION DATA IS AVAILABLE

Puffin Books ISBN 978-0-14-241649-5

Book design by Jeanine Henderson
Text set in Janson

Printed in the United States of America

This book is dedicated to Penny Jordan (1941–2011),
who touched so many people with her words and her kindness.
My life is better from knowing her.

Acknowledgments

I would like to thank my agent Jenny Bent for always helping me find the story, even when I bury it really, really deep! To Christina Phillips and Sara Hantz, obviously I'm a joy to work with, but all the same I would like to thank you for everything. And to Pat for reminding me that this idea would make a good book! To the amazing Karen Chaplin, who has always believed in me even when she's been trudging through all of my amusing little bloopers. Thank you for making me a better writer and for all support and encouragement. And to Kristin Gilson, who stepped in so admirably and whose wonderful sense of humor always makes me smile. Sometimes I think she knows Malik better than I do.

A long overdue thanks to Jeanine Henderson for all the beautiful covers that she has done for my books. I have loved them all and this one is no exception! And to Macey Ward, who looks so much like "my Sophie" that if we ever meet, I will be expecting her to use some magic. Also, a big thank you to everyone else at Puffin, especially the copy editors, who I like to ensure will never want for a job while I'm around.

Another long overdue thank you must go to Allison and Pam Rushby, who both took the time to talk books with me back when the idea of being a published author was just a vague dream. You both made it all seem possible. And finally, to my original Pudding Club buddies, Susan Stephens and Amanda Grange. How lucky were we?

THERE WERE THREE THINGS THAT SOPHIE CAMPBELL knew to be true. First was that the power of positive thinking could make just about anything happen. Second was that Neanderthal Joe was the best band in the world and she didn't care how sold-out their concert was because she and her friends were somehow going to get tickets (see her above thoughts on positive thinking). And the third thing was that if Ryan the biter didn't let go of the brand-new jeans that she planned to wear tomorrow for the first day of sixth grade, then she was going to kill him. Kill him dead.

"I mean it, Ryan, hand them over now and no one will get hurt," Sophie said in what she hoped was a calm and collected manner.

"No." Ryan gave a simple shake of his red hair and wiped his face along one of the legs, causing Sophie to take a deep breath. So much for her calm and collected manner. Seriously, if any of the peanut butter from his face got onto her jeans, there was going to be trouble.

"Why's he doing that?" her best friend Kara wanted to know as she looked up from her sketch pad and wrinkled her brow in confusion. She had only just gotten back from her art camp yesterday and had decided to come along to keep Sophie company while she was babysitting.

"Because he's the devil," Sophie explained as she moved slightly to the left to block Ryan's path.

"Surely he can't be that bad. I mean, he's only six," Kara said in her typical kindhearted way as she put down her charcoal and joined Sophie over by the sofa. "Perhaps he's just playing a game?"

"Oh, it's no game. He really is the ultimate evil. I'm pretty sure I even saw horns," Sophie assured her as Ryan suddenly darted past them and through the open French doors that led out to the extensive garden. They bolted after him.

"Where did he go?" Kara joined her outside, blinking in the bright California sunshine as they both scanned the spacious grounds for any sign of him.

"I don't know. He could be anywhere." Sophie let out a frustrated wail while cursing herself for bringing her precious new jeans babysitting just so that she could show Kara how totally gorgeous they were. It was such a rookie mistake. Especially since every sitter in a three-mile radius knew what a nightmare Ryan was.

Ryan was actually the nephew of her mom's boss, Mr. Rivers, and the only reason Sophie had agreed to look after the little he-beast in the first place was because her mom had bribed Sophie with the brand-new jeans on the way over there.

Well, okay, there was one other reason that Sophie had agreed to do it, but she hadn't bothered to tell her mom about it (since she really had wanted those jeans without having to dip into her Neanderthal Joe savings fund). But the truth was that, in a happy twist of fate, Mr. Rivers lived next door to Jonathan Tait, who was one year older than Sophie and had a habit of practicing basketball in his backyard with no shirt on.

Unfortunately, despite being there for the last three hours, Sophie had seen neither hide nor hair of Jonathan, and even worse, her awesome new jeans were in jeopardy of meeting a gruesome death. All in all, not such a great day. Not to mention—

"There he is," she yelled as she suddenly caught sight of a flash of red hair speeding out from the side of the house before once again slipping past them. Sophie tried to ignore the way he let her jeans trail behind him on the ground. And was that a dirt mark she could see on them? *Oh, he was so dead.*

"Don't worry, Soph. We'll get them back," Kara said as they went racing back through the French doors, Sophie's favorite Vans making a soft padding sound along the hardwood floors. She took the stairs two at a time as Kara followed her. When they reached the top, she looked in both directions. There was no sign of Ryan anywhere, but she soon heard a high-pitched giggle coming from the guest room where he had been staying.

Sophie narrowed her eyes. She would high-pitch giggle him, she decided, as she went charging in there. Ryan was sitting on the large leather chair with his PS3 controls in his hands and an evil smirk on his freckled face. Unfortunately, her jeans were nowhere in sight.

"Where are they?" she asked in a tight voice as she peered under the bed. Kara appeared two seconds later and headed straight for the closet.

"Where are what?" Ryan mimicked in a way that made Sophie long to take his controller and use it to hit him over the head. *Stay calm and think happy thoughts,* she commanded herself. *You don't want to become known as the babysitter who murdered Ryan the biter.* Especially since, while she might not be the biggest fan of kids, she was definitely a fan of extra money, and if she killed Ryan, then she was pretty sure that her babysitting career would be over.

"My jeans, Ryan, where are my jeans?" she asked instead, with as much Zen-ness as she could muster.

"Can't remember." He giggled.

"Perhaps if I hang you upside down by your toenails it will help jog your memory?" she suggested.

"You're not allowed to do that; you're the babysitter," he reminded her, but Sophie just shrugged.

"Well, since I have no intention of ever looking after

you again, I don't really have much to lose. Now tell me: Where are my jeans?"

Ryan paused for a moment, obviously trying to decide if she was bluffing or not before he finally relented.

"Oh, right, *those* jeans. I put them down the laundry chute."

"You did what?" Sophie looked at him blankly since her own house wasn't quite big enough to have a laundry chute, and if she was honest, she wasn't even really sure what one was.

"I think he means that thing." Kara pointed to a small door in the wall, and Sophie felt her breath shorten as she immediately raced over and yanked it open. For a moment all she saw was pitch black as she stared down a long dark tunnel, but as her eyes started to adjust she finally caught sight of something blue lying in a crumpled heap down at the bottom.

Oh, thank goodness!

"I can see them and they're okay. I repeat, they're okay," she called out before spinning back round to where Ryan was still sitting. "So where exactly does this thing end up?" she demanded.

"In the basement, which means... *Hey, where are you going?*" Ryan widened his beady little eyes in surprise as Sophie grabbed Kara's hand and headed for the door.

"The moon. I've heard it's nice this time of year," she snapped in annoyance before tilting her head and glaring at him. "Where do you think I'm going? And you had better hope like crazy that they're not dirty."

"Yeah, well, you're not allowed down there, and if you go, I'll tell Uncle Max," Ryan said, making Sophie realize that he had totally done this on purpose, the little snot. Well, two could play at that game.

"Really, and perhaps I should tell your uncle Max what you did to his cat?" Sophie countered, since she had caught Ryan trying to water the one-eyed tabby earlier. And not in a nice way either.

"I was just playing with him," Ryan's voice started to turn whiny and sullen.

"And the big scratch you put in the back of the walnut desk downstairs?" Sophie arched an eyebrow. "Was that just playing as well? Because my mom works in your uncle's antique store, and I know for a fact that desk is worth over ten thousand dollars. I imagine he would be quite annoyed if he found out you'd ruined it."

"You w-wouldn't." Ryan faltered.

"Wouldn't I?" Sophie said as she shot him a double dose of her world-famous death glare. Okay, so it wasn't really world famous, but she had spent most of the summer practicing it in case Cheryl Lewis gave her any more problems in gym. She must've nailed it because Ryan instantly shut his mouth.

"Fine," he eventually muttered. "I won't say anything."

"Good. And I suggest that you stay here and play your

stupid game because otherwise I just might change my mind about what I tell your uncle Max. Now come on, Kara, let's go get my jeans."

"Wow, he really is evil," Kara said in awe as Sophie raced down the landing toward the wide staircase. "I can't believe he ruined a ten-thousand-dollar walnut desk."

"Actually, I don't have a clue how much the desk cost or what it's made out of," Sophie admitted with a rueful grin. "But I figured he's a six-year-old kid, so he wouldn't know either. The important thing is that it shut him up. Hopefully, he won't give us any more trouble."

"Well, you were very convincing," Kara assured her before suddenly pausing for a moment and frowning. "By the way, what did he mean about the basement?"

"Oh, that. Well, before Mr. Rivers left, he gave me a list of dos and don'ts, and one of them was that no one was allowed in the basement." Sophie shrugged as she reached the ground floor and headed toward the kitchen, where the basement stairs were.

"What?" Kara yelped as a flash of concern raced across her face. "Are you serious? He told you not to go in the basement, and you're still going to do it?"

Sophie, whose fingers were gripped around the basement door, wrinkled her nose. "Well, I can't really get my jeans back if I don't," she pointed out. "Anyway, it will only take a second."

"Yes, but it's a basement." Kara was looking seriously alarmed now. "You know what Harvey says. Going into the basement is the number one cause of death for young American girls. Especially when it's a basement that you've been warned not to go into."

"Kara," Sophie said, groaning. "Harvey was talking about horror-movie clichés—you know he watches far too many of those things. Besides, you don't seriously think I should leave my jeans down there, do you?"

Kara didn't reply, but Sophie could tell by the way her friend was chewing her lip that this was exactly what she did think. Great.

Most people who met Kara Simpson thought that while she was a little bit kooky, for the most part she was sweet and kind and wouldn't say boo to a ghost (though seriously, who in their right mind would say boo to a ghost in the first place? Unless, of course, you wanted to bug the ghost, and in that case you could boo away).

Not that that was the point. The point was that Kara had a stubborn streak that ran through her like a rod of iron. Two rods even. Normally it came out only when she was talking about postmodern art and its use of pop imagery, but occasionally it did make other appearances.

Now was obviously one of them.

Sophie's mom said it was because Kara was an Aquarius and therefore marched to the beat of her own drum, but all Sophie knew was that when her best friend chewed her lip like that, it was hard to change her mind.

"I have to go down there," she repeated in a wheedling voice. "They're my new jeans. *My new jeans that are going to look amazing on me when we start sixth grade tomorrow.* I can't just leave them there."

"Yes, but maybe you could just wait until Mr. Rivers comes home and ask him to get them then?" Kara suggested in a hopeful voice, but Sophie shook her head.

"He's away until later tonight. Ryan is getting picked up by his nanny, who is going to take him back to whatever planet he comes from. But she can't get here until later this afternoon, which is why they needed me to babysit in the first place."

"Well, you could always just wear your other jeans tomorrow. I mean they're cute, too."

They were also covered in pink embroidered flowers and made Sophie look about eight years old. Not exactly how she planned to start sixth grade. Besides, it was okay for Kara—with her long dark hair and her pale green eyes—because she could wear whatever she liked and still look amazing. But for Sophie, with her so-straight-you-could-rule-lines-with-it blonde hair and standard-issue brown eyes, it wasn't so easy.

For a start, she was four feet nothing (and judging from her gene pool, it didn't look like things would be improving anytime soon), so trying to find clothes that didn't make her look young, chubby, or, at the very worst, "cute as a button" was near impossible.

Not that she was complaining, she was just saying that when you weren't America's Next Top Model gorgeous like Kara, you needed to rely on other things to help you get by in life (or, to be more specific, to impress Jonathan Tait).

Hence, her beautiful new jeans, which felt like they were made especially for her. From the moment she had tried them on she just knew that good things would come from owning them. Plus, they somehow managed to make her look taller. Which was why she had no plans at all to leave them trapped on the other side of the basement door.

Those jeans were hers. Somehow the Universe had led her to them, and if she couldn't trust the Universe, then whom could she trust? Sophie felt her resolve strengthen as she twisted the door handle and turned and gave Kara a smile.

"Honestly, I'll be fine. I'll just go get my jeans, and then we can go back upstairs and you can show me the sketch you were doing."

"I don't know." Kara continued to bite her bottom lip in concern. "I still don't like it."

"Kara, relax. I mean, I'll be down there for two minutes tops. Seriously, what could possibly go wrong?"

2

TEN MINUTES LATER SOPHIE HAD FINALLY CONvinced her friend that there were no axe murderers waiting on the other side of the door, and she was able to head down to the basement (though only by sending Kara back upstairs to check on Ryan, just so she would stop calling Sophie back every two seconds just to make sure she was okay).

As she looked around, the first thing Sophie noticed was that, despite what the Declaration of Independence stated, all basements were most definitely not created equal.

The one in Sophie's own house was a dark, musty place that was filled with old toys, loads of her mom's weird pottery statues—which Kara insisted were works of art but Sophie privately thought were just crooked blobs of clay with body parts—not to mention lots of creepy spiders (despite being a very positive person who was at one with the Universe, she drew the line at spiders). Which was why she tended to avoid her own basement as much as possible, venturing down only when she wanted to look at her dad's boxes. Just to make sure they were okay for when he came home.

Whereas the room she was standing in was nothing like that. Instead, it was neat and clean, without a hint of mustiness or spiders.

Over in one corner was a large antique desk that looked even more expensive than the one Ryan had destroyed upstairs. The walls were covered in old paintings whose gilded frames suggested that they also cost loads of money, and for a moment Sophie thought it was a pity that Kara had refused to come down because she would've loved it.

Behind the desk was a floor-to-ceiling bookcase filled with leather-bound books, and dotted around the rest of the room were various display cabinets containing all sorts of old—what her mom liked to call—curios.

This was obviously where Mr. Rivers kept more of his stock from the antiques shop. Then she glanced around again and realized there was no sign of her jeans. For a moment she wondered if Ryan had been playing a trick on her just to get her into trouble, but before she could decide, she caught sight of another doorway.

She headed over and peered in, happy to see that it led into a small, orderly laundry room. Next to the white washing machine and dryer was the chute with a laundry basket sitting below it. Most importantly, her jeans were on the top of the basket.

Sophie immediately thanked the Universe for its help and then snatched the jeans and held them close as she breathed in the scent of denim. Thank goodness that order had been restored to the world.

She headed back to the main part of the basement and was just about to go upstairs to where Kara would no doubt be waiting, when she heard a noise coming from outside.

Because it was the basement, the only windows were set high up on the wall, but when the noise continued, Sophie felt duty bound to find out what it was. She pushed the black leather swivel chair that had been behind the desk over to the window and climbed up.

At first, as she peered out, she thought she was merely looking at Mr. Rivers's side garden, but then she realized that it actually flowed onto the side of the Taits' house.

Sophie widened her eyes. If she had known that there was no side fence between the two houses, she would've spent her entire day out there.

At that moment she heard the noise again and then saw an orange basketball bouncing up and down, before a pair of legs walked into view. She craned her neck upward so she could see the owner of the legs.

Oh, sweet happiness.

It was Jonathan Tait. Sophie pressed her nose up to the glass. Not that she was a pervert or anything, but until a person had seen Jonathan Tait without a shirt on, it was hard to explain just how compelled she was to look at him.

And of course it had to be taken into account that Sophie hadn't seen much of her crush since he had left Miller Road Elementary the previous year to head to Robert Robertson Middle School. But now, not only would she get to see him every day starting tomorrow, she was obviously being given a chance to remind herself just how gorgeous he really was.

See, Sophie knew that her jeans would help her. Wasn't this proof of that? Even if it was in an unusual and slightly weird sort of way.

She grinned some more. Jonathan was just as golden and lovely as she remembered him. All tanned skin, blond hair, and chocolaty brown eyes. But of course the best thing about him was that he was just as lovely on the inside as he was on the outside. Okay, well sure, she hadn't had that many conversations with him—one to be precise. But the point was that it had been a quality one.

It was actually a few months after her dad had first left, simply leaving a note saying that there was something he had to do and that he would be back soon. Problem was that her grandmother, who was staying with them at the time (trying to convince Sophie's mom to stop crying and get out of her pajamas), kept saying that it was obvious her dad wasn't coming back, since no one just vanishes like that unless he really doesn't want to be found. She even used the police report to back up her story.

Hence, a seven-year-old Sophie had been crying her eyes out behind the bike shed. Unfortunately, just as her eyes were at their reddest and her nose was at its snottiest, a gang of fourth graders made their way toward her, and even through her grief, she realized that if they caught her crying, they would probably make her life hell for all eternity.

However, before they could reach her, Jonathan Tait appeared like some sort of modern-day savior, and not only did he pause in front of her to see if she was okay, but he then winked (and she didn't care what Harvey said, it was most definitely a wink, not a facial tic) before he pointed across the practice field to where a fight was taking place. The gang of kids immediately forgot about Sophie and darted away.

That had been four years ago, and it had been love ever since.

Oh, though for the record, Sophie had never cried for her dad again because that very night she had suddenly remembered that her dad never lied to her. Not when she asked him about Santa Claus or even when she asked him if it had hurt when he kicked the wall by mistake when they were playing soccer, and so she didn't care what her grandmother or the police report tried to tell her. If his note said that he was coming back home, then that meant he was coming back home.

Of course, sometimes Sophie thought it would be nice to actually know when he was coming home, since four years was a long time. But the most important thing was after that day she had never lost faith again. Not in her dad and not in the awesomeness that was Jonathan Tait.

Jonathan did another lay-up and Sophie only just resisted the urge to shout and clap out loud (though she was so shouting and clapping on the inside). Instead, she just stood there, holding her jeans up to her mouth in awe as she took it all in.

However, her contented smile suddenly disappeared as she realized that not only was the ball bouncing toward her, but Jonathan had started to jog in the same direction. Sophie gulped. If he bent down and peered over, there was a strong possibility he would notice her looking at him.

As quickly as she could, she started to scramble off the chair. Unfortunately, the movement made the wheels at the bottom go slipping along the concrete floor, and before Sophie quite knew what was happening she found herself falling sideways into one of the antique wooden cabinets nearby.

She flinched as her shoulder slammed into it before she went flying off to one side, where she landed with a thump. *Ouch!* She was just about to get up and check if the cabinet was okay when she realized it was rocking dangerously back and forth.

Nooooooooooooo. She put out her hands to try to stop it from falling over, but it was too late. She barely had a second to think about how it was like something out of one of Harvey's horror movies as the whole thing suddenly went tumbling onto the hard concrete floor (with emphasis on the hard). The contents crashed into a mosaic rainbow of tiny pieces.

Sophie's hand flew to her mouth, and she shut her eyes to will it not to have happened. Like seriously. Unfortunately, the Universe, who had obviously thought it had done quite enough favors for her recently, didn't seem to appreciate her predicament because when she opened her eyes again, she was still completely surrounded by shattered glass and broken curios.

No. No. No.

This was NOT good. Times ten.

And it wasn't like she hadn't been in bad situations before, because she had. For instance, there was the time she and Harvey had been goofing off in science and had accidentally knocked over a beaker of hydrochloric acid and it had eaten a hole into their teacher's briefcase. Or when she and Kara had tried to staple Mrs. Victor's skirt to the chair. But back then all she'd ended up with were a couple of detentions and a boring lecture from her mom. Who knew where this was going to end?

"Sophie, I know you told me to wait upstairs, but I just wanted to see what was taking you so... *Holy freak show.*" Kara suddenly appeared in the doorway, a smudge of charcoal on her nose, her iPod earbuds dangling around her neck, and her jaw almost hitting the floor.

"I know," Sophie groaned. "What a disaster. But the important thing is that we stay calm. I mean, yes, they're all ruined. Like really ruined, but that's not my fault.

Well, okay, so perhaps it was my fault, but honestly, it was an accident. Oh, and maybe I could just blame Ryan, since it's not like he's exactly an angel of goodness."

"Soph—" Kara started to say, her pale green eyes so wide that they would probably out-Bambi Bambi.

"Ack, you're right." She dropped to the ground and frantically started to collect the tiny pieces as her face heated up in panic. "I can't just leave it all here because there's no way Ryan would take the blame for it. Oh, and what if Mr. Rivers freaks out at my mom? I mean, the whole reason she wanted me to babysit was to earn some brownie points, but this is the opposite of brownie points. It's a brownie-point disaster—"

"Sophie." Kara tried again, but she hardly heard as a new idea formed. She regulated her breathing and felt a swoosh of hope go racing through her.

"I could always try and find some replacements before tomorrow. Perhaps my mom could help me? I might have to use up my I Will See Neanderthal Joe in Concert No Matter What Fund, but I think under the—"

"Sophie Campbell. Like, seriously, be quiet," Kara finally cut her off by putting her hand over Sophie's mouth so she could finish the sentence. "I'm not talking about all this broken stuff. I'm talking about that guy over there."

"Muh?" Sophie's reply was muffled as she stared blankly at her friend. "Mhat muy mover mwhere?" she continued before Kara guided her head around and nodded toward the corner of the room. Then she moved her hand from Sophie's mouth. Sophie let out a strangled gasp as she realized that there was indeed a guy over in the corner.

He appeared to be in his late twenties, with brown hair that fell across his dark eyes, and for some obscure reason he was wearing a pair of brightly colored harem pants and no shirt. *Harem pants? Really?*

But the two things that really stood out about him were the fact that his skin was completely orange and the fact that, even though he was sitting cross-legged, he was hovering at least five feet off the ground.

ER, SO, WOULD THIS BE THE RIGHT TIME TO SAY I told you so?" Kara asked in a low voice.

"What?" Sophie squeaked, quite unable to take her eyes off the sight in front of them. "When did you tell me that I'd break a cabinet full of antiques and that a floating guy the color of orange soda pop would suddenly turn up? Because I promise, I would've paid attention if you'd said something like that."

"Fine, so I didn't go into details, but I did try and point out that this whole thing was a bad idea."

"Yes, well, next time perhaps you could be a little bit more specific," Sophie croaked as her heart pounded in her chest like the time she'd drunk three cans of Red Bull in a row.

"I'll try my best," Kara agreed before nervously weaving her fingers together. "So what do we do?"

Run? Scream? Hide? All of the above?

However, before Sophie could even open her mouth to say any of her suggestions out loud, the flying guy suddenly unfolded his legs and floated back down to the ground, where he proceeded to study them with his dark eyes.

"So, which of you two do I have to thank for my release?" he asked as he did a couple of shoulder rolls and then cracked his knuckles.

"Y-your release?" Sophie blinked as she inched closer to Kara while secretly wishing that Harvey was with them, since in order to stop him from spending so much time watching horror movies, his mom had insisted he take up karate last year. Something that Sophie was dearly wishing she had done as well. "R-release from what?"

Oh, and for the record, if he said *mental hospital*, then there was going to be some serious fainting going on.

"From my binding, of course." He used his orange foot to point distastefully to a sliver of red glass that Sophie realized had once been part of a bottle. "I've got no idea how you managed it, but whichever one of you did it, you have my eternal gratitude."

Sophie turned to Kara for a moment and chewed her lip. "Is this making any sense to you? Because I'm lost."

"I've been lost since I realized there was an orange man floating in the air," Kara admitted.

"A man? I'm not a man. I'm a djinn," he corrected with a frown as he started to study the large ring on one of his fingers.

"W-what?" Sophie widened her eyes. "No way. You cannot be serious."

"What's a djinn?" Kara demanded as she turned to Sophie in confusion. "Do you know what he's talk about?"

"Well, yeah. A djinn is like a genie," Sophie was momentarily distracted as she turned to explain it to Kara. "You know, like 'Aladdin and the Magic Lamp' from *The Arabian Nights*. My dad used to read all the stories to me when I was a kid. B-but they're not real. They're just stories. I mean, who would live in a lamp?"

"Exactly." The orange guy nodded in agreement. "For a start, most lamps are made of brass, which always causes me to break out in a rash. Besides, I find that if you're going to stay somewhere, you're better off at the Quality Inn. They have great showers, and I love the free soap and shampoo that you get. As for Aladdin, he wasn't a hero; he was a tyrant. An evil, scum-sucking *sahir* who just happened to have a good publicist." Then he seemed to catch Sophie and Kara's baffled faces, and he let out a morose sigh. "But unfortunately, djinns aren't just a bedtime story. They're real. *I'm* real."

"No. That's not possible." Sophie shook her head, but before she could say anything else, the guy let out another weary sigh and snapped his very orange fingers. The next thing she knew he was no longer orange but a rather Violet Beauregarde shade of blue. He snapped again, and this time his brown hair became a fiery color of red. Snap. He was covered in spots. *Snap.* He suddenly disappeared altogether, and in his place was a large bird with a golden plumage and disturbingly familiar dark eyes. One final snap and Orange Soda Pop Guy was standing in front of them still looking glum.

Say what?

Sophie turned to her friend and tried to speak, but somehow words failed her. Kara seemed to be having an equally hard time figuring out what she should say and they ended up just staring helplessly at each other.

"It's all right." The djinn didn't seem remotely fazed by their reaction. "I'm sort of used to it by now. Humans aren't exactly the most trusting of species, which is why I first developed that little demonstration. I like to call it Introduction to Djinns 101, but if you're still having problems with it, I could always turn into a dinosaur."

Sophie quickly shook her head and let out a sigh of relief as he lowered his snapping hand, since she was pretty sure her brain couldn't cope with any more weirdness right now. Instead, she needed to figure this thing out. And more importantly, make everything go back to normal.

"S-so what are you doing here?" Kara finally asked as Sophie closed her eyes and tried to remember what she knew about djinns. *There was the story of Solomon, who had a famous ring that he used to control loads of djinns.* Unfortunately, the only ring Sophie had on was a plastic flower ring with lip gloss inside it, and she didn't think it could control anything.

"No idea." The djinn shrugged. "All I know is that I was bound to a very ugly glass bottle for the last two hundred years (give or take, since time tends to move a bit differently when you're in a bottle). Problem is, as is often the case, a djinn gets bound to something and once its current owner dies, the thing gets passed along or misplaced, and suddenly you're in hell-bound limbo for eternity. Which, let me tell you, can really screw up your plans for the week."

"Do you mean that Mr. Rivers didn't even know you were there?" Kara asked as she knitted her eyebrows together to consider the notion. *Oh, and then there was the fisherman who tricked the djinn into climbing back into a bottle.* But Sophie quickly dismissed it when she realized that the bottle this djinn had been in was now broken into a zillion pieces.

"I doubt it." The djinn sighed again. "And if you hadn't come along, goodness knows how much longer it might have taken for me to get released."

"You could've been in there forever? That's terrible." Kara, who didn't even like hearing stories of sick kittens, was now staring at him with her pale green eyes filled with compassion.

"Literally. Or worse," the djinn hinted in an ominous voice, but Sophie hardly heard as she suddenly remembered one of her dad's favorite stories. She couldn't remember the name of it, but she could almost hear his voice reciting it in her mind.

Once upon a time, there was a handsome djinn who did a foolish thing and ended up trapped in a bottle. He was in there for a long time, which meant he could do a lot of thinking, and he decided that if he ever got out, he would stop being so foolish. Finally, a human girl came along and opened up the bottle.

The djinn thought she was the most beautiful girl in the world and, completely forgetting his decision not to be foolish anymore, instantly fell in love with her. It was a very bad idea because djinns and humans aren't meant to be together. Then, because she had saved him, the foolish djinn offered her three wishes—

Of course! Sophie felt a rush of excitement go racing through her as she suddenly remembered that the essence of every djinn story was that the person who releases the djinn is granted three wishes. Well, in the case of her dad's story, it was slightly different. *But the human girl, not realizing that the handsome boy was actually a djinn (or that it wasn't wise to fall in love with him) had only one wish. She wished that he would stay with her. And because he loved her and wanted to grant her that one wish, he did.* Which, if you asked Sophie, only proved that each was as foolish as the other.

Not that it really mattered. The important thing was that she wouldn't waste her wishes. Sophie Charlotte-Marie Campbell. Genie releaser. It certainly had a nice ring to it, and she clapped her hands together in excitement, which in turn caused Kara and Orange Soda Pop Guy to look at her.

"You're clapping because he might've been stuck in that bottle forever?" Kara scolded. "Sophie, I'm ashamed of you."

"What? No, sorry, it wasn't that. It's just, I finally remembered something. I mean, he's a genie—"

"Djinn," the orange guy corrected. "You don't call me a genie, and I won't call you a *Homo sapiens*."

"Okay, sorry," Sophie apologized before turning to Kara. "But here's the thing. He's a djinn, and I'm the one who released him. Don't you see what that means?"

"That you're a very nice person?" Kara guessed, but Sophie impatiently shook her straight blonde hair, which felt like it had somehow gone into a static halo around her head.

"No, silly. It means I get the three wishes." Sophie grinned from ear to ear as she started to tick off her fingers. "Okay, so for number one, it will have to be to get this place cleaned up. I mean, it's a bit of a waste of a wish, but I can't let my mom get in trouble. For my second wish, it will be for three tickets to see Neanderthal Joe in concert—complete with backstage passes. And for my third wish. Hmmmm..."

She paused for a minute and considered. Obviously, world peace was tempting, but down at the mall there was also a very cute pair of shoes, which were way out of her pocket-money league. Would that make her a bad person?

Before she could decide Kara coughed and shot her a pointed glare.

"Okay, fine." She let out a reluctant sigh as she forced

herself to lose the mental picture of how adorable those shoes would look with her new jeans. "I suppose you should get one of the wishes, even if you didn't think it was a good idea for me to come in here—but I guess I can't hold that against you." Too much.

"Actually, it's not about the wishes. It's about him. He seems to be shaking his head."

Huh? Sophie spun around and to where Orange Soda Pop Guy was in fact doing a lot of head shaking. And no smiling either.

"Why are you doing that?" she demanded. "Are you saying that I didn't free you from your prison in the bottle?"

"You most definitely did," he assured her. "But that doesn't mean I have to grant you three wishes."

"What? But you said before that you were eternally grateful to me," Sophie reminded him as she once again looked around at all the shattered glass and her excitement started to be replaced by mounting panic.

"And I am," the djinn assured her. "But eternal gratitude and being bound to you for three wishes are two entirely different things. Besides, unless you're an evil scum-sucking *sahir* in disguise and have done a binding spell on me—which, by the way is a rhetorical question, because if you had, then I would be screaming in agony right about now and you would have a very distasteful gloating look on your face—then I'm not obliged to do anything for you."

What?

Well, that couldn't be good news.

Especially since it meant Sophie was right back at the beginning. She was still in a bucketful of trouble and now she had an unobliging djinn to deal with as well. As a person who believed in the power of positive thinking, this was really starting to test her faith. She licked her lips and took a deep breath.

"Okay, so how about just one wish?" she wheedled as she tried to hide her desperation. "You see, while the whole bottle-breaking thing ended up okay for you, the truth is that this isn't my house, and if Mr. Rivers sees this mess, my mom and I will both be in more trouble than you can ever imagine."

"Oh, you'd be surprised at how well I can imagine trouble," the djinn retorted in a dry voice. "And still I can't help you."

"But you have to," Sophie insisted as she decided there was no point in pretending that she wasn't desperate when she absolutely was. "Look, the thing is that my mom's a potter, but on account of losing her mojo after my dad left, she had to go out and get a regular job to help look after my sister and me. Just until my dad comes back home. Problem is that she really sucks at working for other people, and if she loses this job, then who knows how long it will take her to find another one. Which means her boss can't find out that I trashed his basement—by complete accident, I might add. So please, I'll do anything you ask as long as you snap your fingers and make this whole mess go away."

"Anything?" He raised an eyebrow, and Sophie felt a glimmer of hope go racing through her.

"Absolutely." She nodded. "Just name it. Would you like me to explain what's happened in the last two hundred years? Because I don't mean to boast, but I really rock at history. Or perhaps help you buy some more up-to-date clothing—with particular reference to some trousers that aren't bright purple? Or I could even—"

"Wear this ring?" The djinn cut her off as he held out his orange fingers to draw her attention to the hideously ugly large garnet ring that was mounted on some sort of black filigree setting.

"What?"

"You heard me. I want you to wear this ring."

"Are you insane?" Sophie folded her arms and narrowed her brown eyes at him. "I'm not wearing that thing."

"But you just said you would do anything to help your mom," the djinn reminded her. "And I'm not saying you need to wear it forever. Just for twenty-four hours."

"Don't be ridiculous," Kara cut in. "Of course Sophie isn't going to wear your ring. That's so creepy."

"Not to mention ugly." Sophie shuddered as she looked at the revolting thing again. "There's no way in the world I'm putting that thing on. I'm starting sixth grade tomorrow. I don't want to be known as the weirdo girl with the strange ring. People would laugh at me."

"Anyway, *why* do you want her to wear it?" Kara wanted to know.

For the moment the djinn paused before letting out a reluctant sigh. "Okay, the deal is that it's actually the ring that binds me to the bottle. So while this one was kind enough to liberate me from my prison, for the spell to be completely broken, this ring needs to be taken off my finger. By someone who isn't me," he added, obviously concerned that they were both stupid.

"Oh." Sophie nodded. "Well, I'm sorry. If we could help you, we would, but I meant what I said before: I really can't put on some ugly ring just because you want me to."

"So if it wasn't ugly, then you would wear it?" The djinn cocked an eyebrow, but Sophie shook her head.

"Of course not. I mean, how dumb do you think I look? As if I would wear some strange ring for twenty-four hours just because an orange guy tells me to. It's a matter of principle."

"Yeah." Kara nodded in agreement. "What she said."

"And you're sure about this?" the djinn double-checked. "Because it's just, I thought you were keen to get this whole mess cleaned up and to make sure that your mom doesn't get the blame for your mistake. But if I've misread the situation, then—"

"Look, it's not that," Sophie was forced to concede. "I really do need to get this all sorted out, it's just, there's no way I can do what you're asking because... *oh, pretty,*" Sophie suddenly said as the ugly ring disappeared in a puff of smoke and was converted into the most gorgeous silver ring she had ever seen.

It had a wide band and on top was an adorable apple that was completely studded with rhinestones so that it glimmered and glittered like a disco ball.

"What? Oh, this little thing? Did I forget to mention that I could change the shape of it?" The djinn shot her a beatific smile that made his white teeth clash against his orange face. "But of course, if you're not interested, then I—"

"T-tell me again what I would need to do," Sophie said in an enthralled voice as she continued to stare lovingly at the ring. It was even more gorgeous than her jeans. In fact, she was fairly certain that by wearing her jeans *and* the ring together, she would *own* sixth grade.

"If you take this ring off my finger and wear it for twenty-four hours, then I can promise you that not only will I clean up this mess, but you'll never hear from me again."

"Twenty-four hours?" Sophie double-checked.

"That's correct. Oh, and of course the ring is yours to keep once that time is up. So do we have a deal?"

Sophie was about to open her mouth to say "give me the pretty ring already," when Kara glared at her.

"Sophie, no. What happened to your principles?"

"Huh?" Sophie blinked for a moment as she dragged her gaze away from the ring. "Oh, yeah, well, obviously all of that stuff still stands, but the djinn's right. I really have to help my mom. She needs this job. Besides, it's a shiny silver apple ring. How could it possibly be bad?"

"That's probably what Gollum said, and look how he turned out, all wrinkled and crazy." Kara shuddered as she once again demonstrated her stubborn streak. "Besides, what if it's some kind of trick?"

"Yes, but how can it be a trick when he's going to do what I want him to do?" Sophie demanded before turning to him and narrowing her eyes. "Is this some kind of trick?"

"Absolutely not. It will be like this whole thing never happened."

"Really?"

"Really," he agreed. "In fact, you have my word that once you take the ring off me I will disappear forever."

"But not before you clean up the mess," Sophie clarified, just so he knew that she wasn't some stupid eleven-year-old girl who could be duped by an orange djinn.

"That's correct." The djinn gave a regal bow.

"See, Kara, it's a total win/win." She grinned before turning back to the djinn. "I'm in."

"Great." He immediately snapped his orange fingers, and Sophie watched in stunned amazement as thousands of tiny pieces of broken glass, wood, and metal all started to swirl up off the floor into some sort of mini tornado. Next thing she knew the curios were all back together and were once again sitting in the cabinet looking like they'd always been there.

She hurried over and picked up one of the glass bottles that was on the top shelf and started to grin as she realized it was no trick. Next to her Kara was examining a green bowl, and she reluctantly nodded as if she was confirming it was okay. Yes! Sophie barely resisted the urge to punch the air in victory as she turned back to Orange Soda Pop Guy.

"Okay, so why don't you let me have that ring, and then we can pretend that this whole thing never happened."

"It would be my pleasure," the djinn said, and for the first time since Sophie had laid eyes on him, he looked like he was happy.

SOPHIE LIKED TO THINK SHE WAS A POSITIVE THINKER. After all, when Ryan the biter had stolen her jeans yesterday, did she panic? No. Well, maybe a little, but the point was that she had kept a positive attitude and everything had worked out fine.

And when she'd made the big mess in the basement? Again, no panicking. Instead, she had trusted that the Universe would look after her, and it had. *In a totally weird way, of course, but that was neither here nor there; the main thing was it proved her point. She was Miss Positive.*

However, as she crept down the stairs the following morning she had to admit she felt less on the Miss Positive side and more on the Miss Insanely Nervous side, since while she'd managed to avoid her mom yesterday when Ryan's nanny had dropped her home, there was no way she could avoid her this morning. And it wasn't that she didn't want to see her, it was just her mom somehow seemed to have the uncanny ability to read Sophie's mind.

Which, as anyone could imagine, was a little annoying. The worst thing was that Sophie didn't have a clue how she did it, though her favorite theory was that there was a big neon sign above her head that only her mom could read, and it said things like, TODAY I ACCIDENTALLY DROPPED SOME RED PAINT ON YOUR FAVORITE RUG AND I'VE CLEVERLY COVERED IT UP WITH A POTTED PLANT, BUT IF YOU GO LIFT IT, YOU WILL CLEARLY SEE WHAT I HAVE DONE.

And while Sophie was quite happy to accept yesterday's weird run-in with an orange-faced djinn for what it was—good timing—she had a feeling that Mom might not be quite so happy about the whole situation. Especially in regard to breaking all of Mr. Rivers's antiques and then making a deal to have then magically restored.

And so Sophie had decided that apart from not thinking about it, her other best plan of action was simply to avoid her mom as much as possible. Not forever, of course, just until later this afternoon, when the whole thing would be over and the ring would just become a gorgeous rhinestone-encrusted apple that would make anyone who saw it weep with envy. *Because that's what positive thinking was all about.*

In the meantime she had been tempted to take the ring off until it was all over, but the djinn had insisted that she keep it on for at least twenty-four hours, and that if she didn't, he would go back to Mr. Rivers's house and not only break everything again but write her name over the walls as well. Which, if you asked her, was just plain mean. Still, at least he had kept his word, and the minute she had put the ring on, he had disappeared from sight (not even leaving a puff of smoke behind).

She came to a halt at the kitchen door and cautiously peered in. Her mom was hovering over the frying pan while her six-year-old sister Meg was sitting at the table.

"Ah, Sophie, there you are," her mom said without even looking up. See, uncanny. "You're just in time for breakfast, and because you're both starting new schools today, I thought I'd make you something special. Pancakes."

"Great," Sophie said, grateful that her mom hadn't seemed to notice anything weird about her.

"Can't I just have Coco Pops?" Meg asked in a hopeful voice.

"Of course you can't have Coco Pops. You're starting first grade; you need a proper breakfast."

"Well, what if I stayed home? Then I could have Coco Pops," Meg reasoned, but their mom just shook her head, much like she'd done all summer as Meg had waged her campaign to avoid starting first grade. Sophie could've told her little sister right from the start that it wouldn't work, since their mom wasn't only a single parent but she also worked, which meant days off school were few and far between.

"Honey, you're just nervous, but you'll get used to it soon. And anyway, Coco Pops are bad for you—they're full of sugar," their mom said as she carried a plateful of burned pancakes over to the table, and suddenly Sophie understood why her sister had been gunning for Coco Pops. Even the family cat, Mr. Jaws (named by Meg, who, despite having a head of blonde ringlets and navy kewpie-doll eyes, was obsessed by all things that involved killer sharks. Don't ask), was sitting in the sunny part of the kitchen looking uninterested. And he was a cat who had been known to eat his tail.

Sophie halfheartedly put a pancake onto her plate and tried to muster up a smile. When her dad was still around, he used to do all the cooking, and, in fact, it was a running joke that while their mom might have an uncanny ability to read minds, when it came to cooking, her only uncanny ability was to burn water just by looking at it.

Unfortunately, the joke was now on them, since now she and Meg had to eat their mom's cooking every single day, like a constant reminder he wasn't there. The only positive thing that Sophie could get from it was that her mom refused to get any better at cooking because she also knew that he would be coming home soon. That thought had helped Sophie swallow many a burned meal over the last four years.

Then she noticed her mom was staring at her.

"I-is something wrong?" she cautiously asked as she put her hands on her head in case the neon sign really was there and was clearly saying, YESTERDAY I TRASHED YOUR BOSS'S BASEMENT AND THEN MET A MAGIC DJINN WHO COULD FLOAT IN THE AIR AND TURN INTO DIFFERENT SHAPES. OH, AND BY THE WAY, YOU STILL HAVEN'T

FOUND WHERE I SPILLED THE RED PAINT ON YOUR FAVORITE RUG...

"No, you just look different." Her mom frowned for a moment, as if trying to figure it out. "Ah, it must be your new jeans. By the way, Max called this morning, and he wanted to say how pleased he was with the job you did. Apparently, you left the place spotless and even Ryan said that, for a babysitter, you were okay."

"Really?" Sophie, who was just in the process of pretending to eat one of the pancakes, looked up in surprise.

"Yes, really," her mom said before narrowing her eyes. "Why? Were you expecting him to say something else?"

"No. Of course not." Sophie quickly shook her head since she wasn't about to look a gift horse in the mouth (though, to be honest, at her height she would be lucky to look a gift horse in the kneecaps). Anyway, gift horses aside, if Mr. Rivers hadn't said anything and if her mom hadn't done any freaky mind reading, then it meant she was totally in the clear.

And her mom was right about the jeans as well. Sophie did look different in them, and despite yesterday's adventure, there wasn't a speck of dirt on them and they seemed to fit even better than ever. Perhaps she should let her new jeans get kidnapped more often?

"Okay then." Her mom simply nodded as she headed back over to the kitchen counter where she ran some water into the sink. Once upon a time they'd had a dishwasher, but it had broken last year, and they hadn't been able to afford a new one. "And actually, Sophie, while I've got you here, there's something else I wanted to talk to you about. You see—"

However, before she could finish, Sophie caught sight of Kara's head peering through the back door, and so she quickly jumped to her feet.

"Hey, Mrs. Campbell. Meggy." Kara stepped inside and gave them both a broad smile.

"Kara!" Meg brightened immediately; if there was one thing Sophie's baby sister loved more than shark documentaries (why couldn't she just be normal and watch Hannah Montana like everyone else?), it was Kara. Whenever she visited, Meg tended to become Kara's shadow.

"Hi there, Kara." Sophie's mom smiled back. "I've just made some breakfast for the girls, and there's still plenty left if you're feeling hungry."

"Oh, thank you." Kara politely started to head for the table (she didn't like Sophie's mom's cooking any more than the rest of them, but she had better manners). However, before she could sit down, Sophie stepped in front of her and started to drag her back to the door. She loved her friend dearly, but as well as being sweet and kind, Kara was a blabbermouth of epic proportions, and even though Sophie had sworn her to secrecy, she didn't want to put it to the test.

"Actually, Mom, we've got to go."

"Oh." Her mom looked up from the frying pan (where she appeared to be chiseling away the burned remains of the pancakes). "Perhaps you could wait a minute because I really did need to speak to you. And you haven't had your breakfast yet."

"I'll eat it on the way," Sophie lied as she grabbed one, at the same time giving a little prayer of thanks to the Universe that she'd remembered to put some spare granola bars in her bag yesterday. "Besides, we're meeting Harvey down at the corner, and we don't want to be late for our first day."

"I do," Meg chimed up before pouting. However, everyone ignored her.

"Okay, I guess we can talk later. Remember to enjoy yourself," her mom said as she turned her attention back to the frying pan.

"We will," Sophie said as she practically pushed Kara through the door. The minute they stepped outside, Sophie wiped her brow in relief, while at the same time congratulating herself for changing her fitted long-sleeved blouse for a short-sleeved pale green T-shirt. Despite the fact yesterday had been a dull fall day, today the temperatures were soaring. In fact, it was freakishly hot. However, before she could say anything to Kara, her friend turned to her, her eyes wide and full of concern.

"So, did she read your mind and find out about the djinn thing?"

"Shhhhh." Sophie instantly forgot about the weather as she held her finger up to her mouth, since not only was her mom a mind reader, but she had supersonic hearing as well, and you could never be too careful. Finally, they were far enough away. "But no, there was absolutely no mind reading at all. Perhaps she's losing her powers? And even better, Mr. Rivers rang up and said everything was spotless, which means it worked."

"Yes, but I'm still not sure about this, Soph." Kara wrinkled her nose. "I've been thinking about the djinn—"

"Shhhhh," she said again as she caught sight of Harvey loping toward them. His face seemed a bit browner from his trip to Florida but apart from that he looked pretty much the same. His nut-brown hair was still flopping into his eyes, while his long skinny frame seemed to get longer and skinnier by the second. In fact if Sophie had any idea of just how tall he would grow when she'd first met him five years ago, she probably would never have become friends with him since now he only made her look even shorter.

"So," he said the minute he reached them both. "Soph, did your mom read your mind and find out about the djinn thing?"

Sophie immediately turned to Kara and raised her eyebrow. "What happened to not telling anyone?"

"Harvey isn't just anyone," Kara protested. "And anyway he was worried about you as soon as he heard you were babysitting at Mr. Rivers's house. He said he's got weird body language."

"What's wrong with his body language?" Sophie demanded while rolling her eyes. The other thing about

Harvey was that he was a bit of a geeky genius who liked to understand how things worked. And since his folks were on the brink of divorce, he'd started reading a book called *Be Your Own Body Language Expert* so he could figure out what had gone wrong. It was fair to say that both Sophie and Kara were heartily sick of that book.

"Well, I'm not exactly sure," Harvey admitted as they all started to walk toward the bus stop. "But when we were visiting your mom in the store the other week Mr. Rivers was doing some very odd stuff with his hands. According to the book it either means he has an eating disorder or is a serial killer. You should probably tell your mom to get another job and definitely don't do any more babysitting for him. Better safe than hacked up into a million pieces."

"Harvey." Sophie groaned. "That's crazy. And it's also the exact reason why I didn't want Kara to tell you what happened because I knew you would only worry."

"And rightly so, since while I might not have been quite right about the serial killer thing, there is obviously something strange about him if he has an orange djinn living in his basement. Basements are bad."

"But he wouldn't have even known the djinn was in there. You tell him, Kara."

"It's true, Harvey." Kara gave an earnest nod of her head. "The djinn said that once the owner dies, the bottles are just passed on to people who don't have a clue what's in them. He probably just thought the bottle looked pretty and that he could sell it in his store for lots of money."

"I still don't like it." Harvey shook his head so that his hair again went flying into his eyes.

"Well, there's nothing to like or unlike about it," Sophie reminded them both as the yellow school bus pulled to a halt in front of them and everyone started to pile on. "It's all over and done with now and the important thing is that I got my jeans back and my mom never lost her job. Besides, we start sixth grade today and so we really need to lose all the negative emotions and concentrate on making it awesome. I want you to both say after me: 'Today is going to be the best day of our lives.'"

AND TO ALL THE NEW SIXTH GRADERS, WE AT ROBERT Robertson Middle School would like to welcome you and we hope that your time here is a happy one."

"I wonder if she always lifts her eyebrow like that when she talks?" Harvey said in a low voice as they listened to Principal Gerrard talk. "Because I think that means she's telling the truth."

Sophie grinned as she caught her breath. She thought so as well. They had only been in the building for an hour, but already things were looking up. Not only had they all managed to get in the same class but they'd also managed to get Mr. Collins as their homeroom teacher, and everyone knew that he liked to give out candy as spot prizes. The only downside was that they hadn't been so lucky with their lockers and were spread out in all directions, which was why she was trying to catch her breath, since she'd had to sprint to get there on time.

Finally Principal Gerrard stopped talking and said they could all go back to their homerooms. Everyone let out a good-humored boo, and Sophie, Kara, and Harvey started to follow the trail of students back out of the large gymnasium. As they went Sophie rubbed her ears to try to get rid of the buzzing noise that was in them. At first she had thought it was from the principal's microphone, but although the speech was over, the buzzing noise remained.

"Where were you before?" Kara demanded the minute they were free of the crowd and started to head in the direction of their homeroom—well, Sophie hoped it was the right direction, since Robert Robertson Middle School seemed to resemble a rabbit warren with corridors running off in all directions. "I almost thought you were going to be late for the assembly and get a tardy on your first day."

"I know," Sophie sighed. "I swear, my locker is in Siberia. But anyway, you'll never believe who stopped me on the way back to the gymnasium."

"Not Jonathan Tait?" Kara widened her eyes, and for a moment Sophie frowned. If only.

"No, it wasn't that great. But it was a bunch of seventh graders who wanted to know where I got my jeans."

"Why?" Harvey looked at her blankly as he slouched along beside them. Sophie longed to make him stand up straight. Honestly, height was wasted on the tall.

"Because they're awesome," Kara scolded as she hit Harvey in the arm before turning her attention back to Sophie. "So who were they and what did they say?"

"Only Serena Towers and all her friends." Sophie broke out into a grin. She had been dying to tell her friend about it from the moment it happened.

"No way," Kara was suitably impressed.

"Yes, way," Sophie assured her. "And not only did they want to know how much they cost, but when I told them the price, they demanded to know where I got them from because they were so cheap."

"Cheap?" Kara lifted an eyebrow, and Sophie nodded in agreement.

"I know, I wouldn't call them cheap either, but I guess that's seventh graders for you. Anyway, can you believe that a pair of jeans made Serena Towers talk to me?"

"Not really," Harvey looked at them both blankly, but the two girls ignored him.

"That's amazing." Kara's green eyes were wide with excitement. "And I've got some even more amazing news."

More amazing than having some seventh graders ask where you got your jeans? Sophie didn't think so.

"It is pretty good," Harvey confirmed, and Sophie looked at them both with interest as Kara discreetly pulled out her cell phone and held the screen up for Sophie to read the text message (while she tried to ignore the fact that she was probably the only sixth grader whose mom refused to buy her a cell phone. Honestly, it almost bordered on being criminal).

"*Nth Joe r releasing xtra txs 4 concert. location deets 2come,*" Sophie read out loud before turning to her friends in astonishment. "Are you serious?" But even as she said it, she suddenly realized that all around them was the soft buzz of text messages being sent and received. The news was obviously spreading like viral wildfire, and it was obviously very, very real. They might've missed out on the first round of Neanderthal Joe tickets, but there was no way they were going to miss out this time.

Sophie turned and grinned to her friends. See, she knew that sixth grade was going to rock.

By lunchtime Sophie was in heaven. Not only had she received a gazillion more compliments about her jeans, but when they'd gone to the library to get shown around, she had spotted Jonathan Tait just behind the nonfiction shelves. Sophie had instantly made herself busy in that same section, grabbing as many books as she could possibly hold as she listened to him talking to his friends about the Neanderthal Joe concert. Seemed Sophie, Kara, and Harvey hadn't been the only ones who had missed out on tickets first time around, and while no one knew where the tickets would go on sale, they would be getting a location text about it tomorrow. Bring on tomorrow.

Unfortunately, before Sophie could dump the books one of the librarians found her and instantly dragged her over to demonstrate how the self-checkout machines worked, which explained why she now had eight heavy shark books in her bag. At least her sister would be happy.

"Okay," Harvey announced as they walked down the

corridor. "According to what I've heard, the cafeteria only seats three hundred people, and there are five hundred and fifty kids at the school. So if we're not quick, we'll have to sit outside or on the ground."

"I don't think that means we need to jog there," Sophie complained as he started to lope ahead of them in long strides, a serious expression plastered across his face. Not that she was really surprised, since the only thing Harvey liked more than watching horror movies and studying nonverbal body language was eating. In fact, he liked eating more than anything in the world, and sometimes, when he was super hungry, he had even been known to eat Sophie's mom's cooking without complaint.

"Yes, we do," he insisted. "Because if we don't put a claim in on Day One, then we'll be stuck outside for the rest of the year. I mean, think about it: this isn't fifth grade anymore, which means all the rights that we had are now gone. We're the bottom of the barrel. So come on, Soph, stop dawdling—unless your precious new jeans can also get you a seat at the cafeteria?"

"I'm not dawdling," Sophie protested as she felt her shoulder sag under the weight of her eight shark books. *And as it goes, her precious new jeans probably could get them a table.* "Look, you guys go on ahead and save me a seat. I'm going to dump these things off before I turn into the Hunchback of Notre Dame."

"Do you want me to come with you?" Kara checked, but Sophie shook her head.

"No, it's all good. I should manage to find my way there and back."

"Well, we'll see you soon then," Kara said as Harvey practically dragged her down the corridor and Sophie made her way to her new locker as fast as her stupid heavy bag would let her.

She finally reached it and quickly put her books away. Then she caught sight of her favorite affirmation that she had taped up in her locker earlier that morning. *Everything will work out just the way I want it to.* Sophie grinned. That was for sure. Then she started to fan her face. Boy, it was hot in here. She started to wonder if the boiler was broken, because—

Psssst.

Huh. Sophie spun around, but apart from a group of boys down the other end, the corridor was empty. Okay, so that was odd. Perhaps it was because she was hot, and hungry, and—

Psssst.

There the noise was again, and this time when she looked up she caught the briefest glimpse of what looked like purple harem pants before they disappeared behind the side of the lockers.

No. Sophie only just stopped herself from wailing out loud. *Seriously, no.*

She felt her heart start to pound as she forced herself to walk around the corner. There was no one there, but the door to the nearby janitor's closet was half open.

Despite all her instincts, she stepped in, and her worst fears were confirmed when she caught sight of the djinn lounging on an upside-down mop bucket, flicking through a magazine. For some unknown reason he was no longer orange, more a gray-white color. He also didn't appear to be miserable anymore.

More of the *no, no, no.*

"Oh, hey, there you are." He beamed as he put down his magazine and gave her a cheery wave. Sophie ignored it as she stared at him in horror.

"I don't understand."

"I was starting to wonder if you hadn't heard me," he continued in a merry voice that was nothing like the way he had been last time they'd met.

"What are you doing here? I thought we had a deal. You would fix the mess; I would wear the ring; and then I'd never have to see you again," she reminded him as she waved her hand in the air to show him that she was still wearing it. "You were pretty specific about it."

"That's right." The djinn nodded. "By the way, nice jeans. They really make you look taller."

"You think so? Thanks," Sophie said before realizing what he was doing. "Hey, stop trying to change the subject. What are you doing here?" As she spoke, she started to blow some cool air onto her face, since the janitor's closet was even hotter than the rest of the school.

"Okay." The djinn licked his un-orange lips. "The thing is, while guilt isn't normally an emotion I can relate to—I mean, you live for a couple thousand years, you're bound to do some not-so-nice stuff, and really what's the point of letting it eat you up inside? But for some crazy reason I've been feeling bad about everything, so I thought that before we get started, I should apologize."

"Apologize for what?" Sophie stared at him blankly before wrinkling her nose. "And why aren't you orange anymore?"

"Okay, so it looks like you haven't figured it out yet, which means I'm going to have to explain it to you." The djinn seemed to be busy studying his fingernails before finally looking up at her. "You see, the reason I'm not orange anymore is because I'm no longer a djinn. When you took the ring off me, you killed me."

"I did *what*?" Sophie stared at him in horror since, as a rule, she didn't even like squashing bugs, and no matter how annoying Orange Soda Pop Guy was, she certainly didn't want to kill him (well, okay, perhaps just a little bit, but only in her mind, not like for real or anything).

"You killed me," he repeated before shooting her a reassuring smile. "Oh, but don't get me wrong. The killing part is great. I wanted you to kill me, since you have no idea how hard it is to off yourself when you're immortal. The only problem is that the stupid Djinn Council is all worried about our reducing numbers, which means they get really cranky if we don't pass on our inheritance. You know, an eye for an eye, a djinn for a djinn, and all of that malarkey. Though, between you, me, and the wall, they're a bunch of old women. So anyway, that's where you come in."

"Still not following. Are you trying to tell me that you're giving me this ring as an inheritance? I thought you'd already given it to me." Sophie furrowed her eyebrows and tried to keep up, but honestly, this was getting more complicated than Mr. Harris's fifth-grade math class.

"It's not exactly the ring that I've given you. It's my powers. Well, not all of them, because while I don't like to boast, I was pretty strong. But you've got a lot of them. In fact, you should think of it like a gift set. Ring and power all tied up in one nice, nifty little package." The djinn shot her a hopeful smile. "Of course, the downside is that not everyone takes to it and the power can kill them, but the good news is that you survived. Yay, you!"

"Okay, so there is entirely too much talk about death and killing in this conversation. First I killed you, and now you tried to kill me?"

"Yes, but again, the important thing to remember is that the ring didn't kill you. Which is a very good thing."

"But *why* is it a good thing?" Sophie wrinkled her nose as she heard a group of kids walk by outside, arguing about who had the best Guitar Hero score. "I still don't understand what you're trying to say."

"In a nutshell, I'm trying to welcome you to your new and very long life." He gave her an encouraging smile. "As a djinn."

6

MY NEW LIFE AS A *WHAT*?" SOPHIE NEARLY YELLED, remembering just in time that she was in a janitor's closest of Robert Robertson Middle School. *But what?*

"A djinn," the djinn replied helpfully. "And you don't need to look so concerned, because I can assure it's not that bad. It's fun even."

"Well, if it's so much fun, then why did you want me to take off your ring and kill you?" Sophie pointed out as she waved her arm in the air.

"Ah, nice deflection." The djinn nodded his head in approval. "And yes, you're right. I was a bit... *tired*... of it all, but I can assure you that you won't feel like that for a very long time. Anyway, we can talk about that later, because now that you know how sorry I am, we need to get started. You see, as the djinn who created you, it's my duty to teach you how to use your newfound powers. In fact, the Djinn Council members are sort of sticklers for it. I need to show you the ropes, and once they're satisfied with the job I've done, then they will consider rewarding me. With big shiny things. So first we need to concentrate on—"

"No," Sophie suddenly put her hands over her ears.

"What are you doing?"

"It's called not listening. You should ask my teacher from last year because apparently it's something I'm very good at."

"Yeah, well, unfortunately, that's not going to make me go away."

"Yes, it will. I'm a very positive person, and when I wish for something to happen, it does. So I'll just keep not listening and wishing until it happens."

"Don't say that." The djinn suddenly looked concerned.

"Say what? That I wish you would go away? Why? Will it work?"

"Unfortunately, yes."

"Good, well then, I wish you would go away."

The djinn seemed to mutter something under his breath as he started to fade from sight. "Look, when you need me to come back, just clap your hands. Like this." Then after giving three claps he disappeared all together.

For a moment Sophie just stared at the empty space before it sank in that he had really gone.

And not soon enough. After all, what was the point of promising someone you would never bother her again if you kept turning up and bothering her?

The important thing was that she had gotten rid of him, and so, without a backward glance, she hurried out of the closet and back down the corridor toward the cafeteria.

"Where have you been?" Kara demanded the moment Sophie sat down. "It's been a nightmare holding this chair for you. These kids are piranhas. And why do you look like that?"

"Okay, so don't freak out, but you know that thing we weren't going to talk about anymore?"

"What thing?" Harvey looked up from the piece of pizza before he suddenly started to choke. "Oh, no, you don't mean the dj—"

"Shhhhh." Sophie held her finger up to her lip to silence him as she cautiously glanced around. Thankfully, everyone seemed to have better things to do than listen in on their conversation, and so she reluctantly nodded her head. "But yes, that thing."

"What about it?" Kara said in alarm as she stopped working on the sketch of Harvey that she'd been doing. "It hasn't done something, has it?"

"Yes, it's done something," Sophie yelped in annoyance. "Can you believe it turned up here? At school."

"What?" Harvey automatically put his hands into a Kung Fu pose and looked around. "Where is it?"

"It's not here now," Sophie informed him as she reached out and lowered his hands back to the table. "I got rid of it."

"You did?" Harvey widened his eyes from underneath his long bangs. "How?"

"With the power of my mind. Seriously, you should never underestimate the value of positive thinking. I just said I wished it would go away, and it did."

"But what was it doing here in the first place?" Harvey looked confused. "I thought you made some sort of weird deal with it."

"Exactly." Sophie nodded her head. "We *did* make a deal, and I kept my end of the bargain but he didn't keep his. And I tell you what, he'd better not turn up again, or else he really will feel the full force of my mental powers."

"Yes, but I still don't understand *why* he came back." Kara frowned as she unthinkingly drew a tiny portrait of the djinn on the sketchbook in front of her. Then, once she realized what she'd done, she immediately scribbled over it.

"Oh, well would you believe he was trying to tell me that by wearing his ring, I am now a djinn." Sophie rolled her eyes. "Oh, and get this. He even said that I was lucky because sometimes the power of the ring kills people. I mean, seriously."

"What?" Harvey and Kara both yelled as one, causing several heads to turn and look at them with interest.

"Guys, shhhhh." Sophie glared at them. "This is our first day of sixth grade; we don't want to stand out too much. Anyway, he was lying, of course. Perhaps it's some weird djinn joke they do? Like *America's Funniest Home Videos* but for orange people? By the way, can you guys hear that weird buzzing noise?" Sophie paused and rubbed her ear to get rid of the strange static noise that had been bugging her all morning.

"I can't hear anything." Harvey chewed his lip and looked concerned.

"Me either." Kara shook her long hair. "And how do you know the djinn was lying?"

"Actually, that would be quite easy to tell," Harvey cut in. "Since his nonverbal signs would clearly give him away. Did he flare his nostrils at all or avoid eye contact? Those are always good indicators."

"Strangely enough, I was too busy freaking out to notice what his nostrils were doing or where he was looking," Sophie retorted, while deciding to ignore the weird buzzing noise in her ear. Meanwhile, her friends were both looking worried.

"So how do you know he wasn't telling the truth then?" Kara persisted.

"Well, Exhibit A is the fact that I'm not a djinn," Sophie pointed out, her voice not much more than a whisper. "I mean, I thought that was obvious. Anyway, the thing is, I've decided that from now on we're probably best not to mention it ever again. Let's just pretend it never happened. Especially the—"

"Hey, you. Are you Sophie Campbell?" a voice suddenly said, and Sophie turned around in her seat to see

Melissa Tait standing behind her with her hands on her hips.

Could this day get any weirder?

Melissa was Jonathan Tait's twin sister, but while everyone loved Jonathan, who was nice and easygoing (and super easy to look at) his sister was a completely different kettle of fish.

In fact, when she had graduated from Miller Road Elementary the year before, even the teachers had looked relieved that she was going. Sophie just tried to avoid Melissa in order to stay under her Queen of Mean radar.

"Well? Is that your name?" Melissa repeated (in a way that suggested she didn't like to repeat herself) before she flicked a perfect, glossy strand of blonde hair back from her shoulder. "Because I want to talk to you. About your jeans."

"Oh, right," Sophie finally replied after Kara had given her a gentle nudge in the ribs and she awkwardly got to her feet. It was one thing to attract the attentions of Serena Towers and her friends, but for her jeans to attract Melissa's attention was something else entirely. Since even though nearly everyone was afraid of her, there was no denying that she had the best taste ever. People even said she would probably get a job at Teen Vogue when she was older.

"So kids have been talking about them all morning," Melissa said as Sophie obligingly stepped closer to her and wrinkled her nose. She knew that the Universe had wanted her to buy the jeans to help her get closer to Jonathan Tait, though she hadn't quite imagined it would be by way of his scary sister. Still, who was she to question the Universe?

"I got them at that store at the back of the mall, Jean-I-us," Sophie said in a helpful voice as she gave her ear another rub to try to dislodge the buzzing noise that was still racing around.

"Really?" Melissa arched an eyebrow that looked suspiciously like it had been shaped. "Because I don't believe you."

"What?" Sophie blinked. "B-but I did. You can ask my mom because she was with me. N-not that I always go shopping with my mom, of course, but it was on a Sunday and there weren't many buses, and then she had to drop me off to babysit, so we went together. Just this one time—"

"Enough. I know the place, and I can assure you that they don't sell two-hundred-dollar Motion jeans there. In fact, the only place that sells these jeans is Bella's Boutique, and unless you've been on the waiting list for them, you still wouldn't get a pair. *Were you on Bella's Boutique's waiting list for them?*"

Sophie shook her head while next to her she could vaguely see Kara clutching nervously at Harvey's arm.

"No, but—"

"However," Melissa continued. "I will tell you where you *were.* You were next to my house yesterday babysitting that brat of a kid, and you paid him to come and take my jeans from the clothesline and leave me with a cheap knock-off pair."

"What? No—"

"No, you weren't next to my house yesterday?" Melissa raised her eyebrow again. Definitely shaped. How else could she make them go like that?

"I mean, yes, I was babysitting yesterday, but no, I didn't take your jeans off the line," Sophie said in a bewildered voice as she dragged her gaze away from Melissa's perfect eyebrows. "Why would I?"

"You tell me." Melissa gave an impatient snort.

"Well, I didn't," Sophie insisted before pausing for a second. "I mean, Ryan, the kid I was babysitting, did run off with my jeans, but I certainly never told him to go and swap them with yours. And if he did—"

"Okay, so I'm going to stop you there because this is getting boring. The point is, you've got my jeans on and I want them back."

"But—" Sophie started to say, but this time it was Kara who cut her off with a nervous cough.

"Actually, the label on the back does say Motion."

"What?" Sophie immediately twisted around and then let out a long groan as she saw an unfamiliar label staring back at her. How on earth could she not have noticed? But even as she thought about it, she knew the answer. It was because she had been so distracted with the whole orange djinn thing that she hadn't really looked closely at what she now realized were a pair of designer jeans. She swung back around to where Melissa was still glaring at her.

"I-I didn't realize." She felt her face start to get warm. "Look, Melissa, I'm sorry. Really, really sorry. Ryan must've swapped them."

"You think?" Melissa tapped her shoe impatiently on the floor. "But what I want to know is, What are you going to do about it?"

"Oh, right." Sophie's face got even warmer. "Well, I guess I'd better give them back to you," she started to say, before realizing that she couldn't very well give them back since she didn't have anything else to wear, and naked wasn't really the way she had planned to start sixth grade. "Perhaps tomorrow?"

"You think I want them back after you've squeezed your thighs into them?" Melissa let out a delicate shudder. "Not likely, but since you owe me, tomorrow you'd better bring me two hundred dollars so I can buy a new pair. Got it? Oh, and before I forget, if you don't give me the money, you can kiss your reputation good-bye, because I will make sure that every single person in the school hears about this little episode. Are we clear?"

Then, without waiting for an answer she turned around and stalked away from where Sophie was still standing.

"Two hundred dollars? *Two hundred dollars?*" Sophie groaned as she finally sank back down into her chair. "That's all my Neanderthal Joe ticket money (not to mention a program and a tour T-shirt). Talk about a catch 22, because if I don't give her the money, then she'll ruin me. Like really, really ruin me. But if I do give her the money, then I'll have to miss out on what is sure to be the greatest concert in the world, which will also ruin me. This is the worst thing ever."

Then she realized that neither Harvey nor Kara was saying anything, so she lifted an eyebrow at them.

"You know, this is the part where you both tell me it's not that bad. Perhaps remind me of hungry kids in Africa so that I can put it all in perspective," Sophie prompted them as they continued to stare at her. "What? Why are you both looking at me like that?"

"Okay, there's something you should know, but I don't think you're going to like it," Harvey said.

"I've just been humiliated in front of the entire cafeteria by Melissa Tait; I'm pretty sure I can take it."

Harvey licked his lips and pushed away his pizza crust. "So you might want to take a look at your fingers. And your arm."

"What?" Sophie loved Harvey, of course she did, but sometimes she feared for his sanity. "Is this another one of your nonverbal communication things? Because it's not funny."

"Soph," Kara said in a soft voice as she continued to stare. "He's not joking. You really need to look at your arm."

Sophie shot them both a look before she cautiously peered down at her arm (which, thanks to this boiling weather and her short-sleeved T-shirt, was almost fully exposed). Then she only just resisted the urge to scream as she looked at her other arm and realized her friends really hadn't been joking.

As far as she could make out, she was completely orange.

7

OKAY, SO IS ANYONE ELSE THINKING WHAT I'M thinking?" Harvey asked ten minutes later as they squeezed into the janitor's closet, which was full of mops and buckets but completely empty of evil, lying djinns who obviously liked to spend their days tricking innocent girls.

"What? That this place smells of bleach?" Kara wrinkled her nose as she looked around the tiny space. But Sophie hardly heard them as she continued to stare at her arm in disbelief.

There had been moments in her life when she had really thought the world was about to stop. Like when her dad had left and then forgotten to come back, or when her mom had refused to get out of her pajamas for four weeks after it had happened. But nothing had prepared her for how she might feel to discover that she was orange.

Oh, and she wasn't talking about a "spray-tan-gone-wrong" sort of orange either, but more of a "Hello, and welcome to your new life as an Oompa Loompa" orange.

"No." Harvey shook his head so that his straight hair went flying into his eyes. "Of course I'm not talking about the smell, I'm talking about Sophie. Is anyone thinking that the djinn wasn't lying about the fact that Soph's now got all of his power?"

"But that's ridiculous." Sophie finally dragged her gaze away from her arm and resisted the urge to look into the small chipped mirror that was hanging on the wall, since absolutely no good could come from seeing her face right now. "I mean, it makes no sense. *And where is the djinn anyway?* He said all I had to do is clap and he would turn up. Why hasn't he turned up? Why?" she demanded as she continued to clap her hands in a manic beat.

"I don't know, but the important thing is not to panic," Kara said in a soothing voice.

"How can I not panic?" Sophie panicked as she started to clap even louder. "I'm orange."

"Yes, but for all we know it could just be some weird disease with a really complicated name and we're freaking out about nothing," Kara said. "What if we go to the school nurse and ask her?"

"You think a disease that turns you orange isn't something to freak out about?" Sophie yelped, and Kara shot her an apologetic wince.

"Sorry. I just meant that it might be a complete coincidence and nothing to do with the djinn at all. Stop looking at me like that, Harvey. It could happen."

"I really don't think that there are many diseases in

suburban San Diego that turn you orange." Then he turned back to Sophie, the frown lines still clearly etched into his face. "So when you saw the djinn before, what exactly did he say to you?"

Sophie rubbed her brow for a moment and tried to recall. Of course the problem with being a positive person was that she tended to push aside the negative stuff that she didn't want to hear (especially when it involved being turned into a djinn).

"Okay, so first he told me that by taking the ring off his finger, I had killed him. Then he said that because I'd worn the ring for twenty-four hours (without dying), I'd now inherited all his powers. I mean, can you believe that?" As she spoke she blew another breath of air up onto her burning forehead.

"Yeah, sort of." Harvey reluctantly nodded while ignoring the blatant glare that Kara was throwing at him. "I hate to say it, but it sounds like he was telling the truth."

"Oh, man, this is bad." Sophie helplessly waved her hands in the air before realizing that seeing her orange fingers was anything but comforting. She immediately thrust them into her pockets instead. "I mean, I'm eleven. What am I going to do?"

"Go back in time and not put the ring on?" Harvey suggested.

"Harvey, you're not helping," Kara interrupted, but Sophie shook her head and felt a faint glimmer of hope rise up.

"Actually, he's right. Well, not about the going back in time thing, but it all started with the ring, so what if I just take it off? Perhaps things will just go back to normal?"

Please let things go back to normal.

"I don't know." Kara started to frown. "Didn't the djinn tell you to leave the ring on? I mean, things are bad enough. You don't want to make them worse."

"Worse? How can it get worse? Besides, he also told me that I would never see him again and that everything would be fine, so I guess we can conclude that the djinn is a big fat liar, complete with flaming pants and a very long nose," Sophie retorted as she closed her eyes (to stop from noticing how pretty and shiny the ring was). Then, before she could change her mind, she yanked it off her finger.

There, it was done, and now her life could go back to normal and... *argh.*

She dropped to the floor in pain as it felt as though a thousand daggers were plunging into every inch of her skin.

"What's happening?" Kara yelled in alarm. But Sophie hardly heard her as her mind clouded with pain, and she shut her eyes to try and close it out.

"Soph, put the ring back on," Harvey commanded, but when she didn't respond, he bent down and eased it over her knuckle. The pain instantly retreated, and Sophie looked up at him, her mind still a bit foggy.

"Oh my God," she croaked. "That *was* worse. Like really, really worse." Then she leaned against the mop bucket as the truth finally hit her. She let out a groan. "I'm a djinn, aren't I?"

This time even Kara reluctantly nodded her head. "It seems like it."

"B-but I don't want to be a djinn." She could feel her lip start to wobble. "Especially not an orange one. How can I even leave the closet looking like this? I'll tell you how, I can't. Which means I'll have to live here. Forever. With only a mop and a bucket for company. I'll be like Tom Hanks in that movie where he's stuck in an airport with only a coconut to talk to, but at least he wasn't orange and—"

"That was an island, not an airport," Harvey interrupted, but Sophie just waved him off.

"Whatever. The point is that I can't let anyone see me like this. You know how kids are. I would *never* be able to live it down."

"Yes, but if you're a djinn, perhaps you can do some magic and become un-orange?" Kara suggested. "I mean, when we saw the djinn yesterday, he was doing all sorts of stuff without even breaking a sweat."

"Yeah, like tricking me into wearing his stupid ring," Sophie brooded before realizing that right now freaking out wasn't going to get her anywhere. "But I guess I could try."

Harvey frowned. "I'm not sure that's such a good idea, but if you are going to try and dabble with forces beyond your control, I don't suppose you could magic me up some food as well? We had to leave the cafeteria pretty quick, and I didn't get to finish my lunch."

"Harvey," Kara growled.

"What? I'm just saying that a little food wouldn't go astray. I mean, it's not like you couldn't ask her for something as well. One of those horsehair paintbrushes that you're always going on about. Or...okay, fine. I'll stop thinking about food," he trailed off, probably influenced by the way Kara had narrowed her normally wide eyes at him.

"Thank you," Kara said in a sweet voice before giving Sophie a reassuring nod. "Just focus on thinking unorange thoughts."

"Okay." Sophie took a deep breath. After all, not only was she a positive thinker, but she was also a master of visualization. And despite the fact that her vision of the first day of sixth grade wasn't quite going as planned, Kara was right, if she really was a djinn, then it stood to reason that she could do magic.

Which, she had to admit, would be very cool.

She cleared her mind and tried to picture what her face normally looked like (okay, without so many freckles, but what was the harm in that?), and then she tried to regulate her breathing. Slowly, her mind emptied, and she shut her eyes and let herself get lost in the moment.

I'm not orange. I'm not orange. I'm not, not, notty-not-

not orange, she mentally chanted as a feeling of peace settled over her. Finally, after what seemed like ages, she opened her eyes and turned to her friends.

"Well?" she demanded in an expectant voice. "How do I look?"

"You know, it seems to have gone a little bit paler," Kara said in a kind voice.

"Really?" Sophie wanted to know as she finally succumbed to the temptation of looking at herself in the mirror. It was not pretty viewing, and the combination of her straight blonde hair, her brown eyes, and her freckles all against the backdrop of her bright orange skin made her look like a bad fall day.

"Okay, not really," Kara was forced to concede as she put her hand over the mirror so that Sophie would stop staring at her reflection. "But perhaps these things just take time to learn?"

"Which wouldn't be a problem if we didn't have a math class in ten minutes," Harvey said as he glanced at his watch, and Sophie immediately shook her head.

"I'm sorry, guys, but there is no way I'm leaving this closet looking like this."

"You want to miss class on your first day of school?" Harvey asked.

"I don't exactly have much choice." Sophie waved her arms to prove her point, but before she could say anything else, Kara let out a yelping noise.

"Actually, I think I've got an idea of how we can get rid of the orange skin."

"You know magic?" Harvey looked surprised, but Kara quickly shook her head as she rustled around in her bag for something.

"Not exactly." Kara grinned. "I was thinking more along the lines of painting you."

"You want to *what* me?" Sophie stared at her friend as if she was crazy. *Actually, scrap the "as if"' part of that sentence.*

"Seriously, this paint I got at my art camp is amazing, and it's totally nontoxic, so it will be fine on the skin. Now hold back your hair so I can start on your face."

"What? No, it's bad enough being orange. I don't want to be orange and covered in paint," Sophie protested.

"How about being orange and given a detention for missing your afternoon classes on the first day of school," Harvey pointed out. "It's got to be worth a try. At least until your djinn friend turns up and teaches you a few tricks."

"Come on, guys," Sophie started again. "You don't seriously think this is going to work, do you?"

"It would work a lot better if you could keep still," Kara admonished with a frown as she chewed on the end of her paintbrush for a moment before using it to carefully dab Sophie's chin. "Because if you keep wriggling, I'm going to get paint all over your clothes."

"I know, but I can't help it." Sophie moaned some more. "I mean, this is the worst thing ever. And why hasn't the djinn turned up yet?" she demanded as she once again clapped her hands together.

"I don't know, but I do know that you need to stop with all the clapping and let Kara finish painting you," Harvey said.

Personally, Sophie would've preferred to go straight home and hide under her bed until this whole thing was sorted out, but they were right, sneaking out of school on the first day probably wasn't such a great idea. Especially since her mom had been looking a little bit stressed lately and her getting a detention probably wouldn't help. *For that matter, neither would finding out that her daughter had been turned into an orange djinn.*

"Okay, I'm almost finished." Kara stepped back and seemed to be examining Sophie's face with a critical eye before turning her attention to Sophie's hands and arms. Finally, she nodded in approval. "There. Done. And you know, as long as you don't let anyone get too close to you, I think you should be okay for the next two classes."

"And this will help cover you up," Harvey added as he shrugged off his favorite hoodie and draped it over her shoulders.

"Thanks," Sophie said as she wriggled into it. Due to the fact that Harvey was so tall (and she was so short), it reached almost to her knees, and the sleeves covered not only her arms but her hands and fingers as well. "Though I'm still not sure about this."

"It won't be forever." Kara gave her shoulder a reassuring squeeze as she passed over a small mirror so that Sophie could inspect her face. It wasn't perfect, but at least the paint was now hiding the worst of the orangeness. Then she inspected her fingers and wrists and tried to convince herself that they looked normal. "It just needs to work until you can get hold of the djinn and get this whole thing sorted out. Now, there's the final bell, so we'd better get our hustle on. Oh, and Soph, one more thing."

"What?" Sophie blinked as she tried not to think about just how insane this day was becoming.

"Don't let anyone throw water on you."

Yup, definitely insane.

WOW, I CAN'T BELIEVE THAT REALLY WORKED," HARvey marveled a couple hours later as the three of them piled off the school bus and congregated in a huddle on the pavement in the dull September afternoon. "I mean, no one said *anything* about the fact you were covered in paint or that you were wearing a hoodie that came down to your knees. Sixth grade really is different."

"What do you mean?" Sophie looked at him in alarm. "You told me you were sure it would work. That's why I let you guys do it in the first place."

"Yeah, but come on, Soph. You're orange and you're covered in Kara's kooky paint. You didn't really believe me, did you?"

"Not anymore I don't," Sophie squeaked as she pulled out the small mirror and inspected her face again before realizing that there were still a few seventh graders loitering around them. She quickly thrust her hands deep into her pockets again. At least the buzzing in her ears had stopped, but she was still boiling hot.

"Sophie looks completely natural. *And there's nothing kooky about my paint either,*" Kara added with a sniff.

"Hey, don't get me wrong," Harvey quickly protested. "I'm happy it did work, it's just, I was worried. Especially when she put her hand up to answer Mr. Langden's question about who first used bronze in their society and her sleeve slid up so you could see her orange elbow."

"Yes, that was a mistake," Sophie was forced to agree as they turned and started to walk toward her house. "But it was just when everyone else was getting the answer wrong, I couldn't quite help myself. I mean, who doesn't know it was the Mesopotamians?"

"Er, me," Harvey admitted before turning to them both. "So what now? Do you want to practice your new skills or anything like that?"

"Harvey, if you're trying to convince her to magic you up some food again, then you can just—"

"Hey, of course I'm not. I have Cheetos." Harvey looked offended, while at the same time obviously remembering that he really *did* have his favorite snack food. He instantly started to rummage around in his bag and pulled out a slightly squished packet. "I was just trying to be helpful."

"And that's very kind of you," Sophie assured him while waving off his offer of a Cheeto (for which he looked heartily relieved). "But the thing is that I don't need to practice anything because I've figured out a new plan," Sophie confided while trying to resist the urge to grin, since, as far as she could tell, the idea that she'd come up with in her in math class (after she'd spent half an hour trying unsuccessfully to make her pencil lift off the table) was pretty much flawless.

Not that she was really surprised; after all, her dad had always taught her that the secret to success was all in the planning, and that even a bad plan was better than no plan. Which meant that Sophie had been coming up with plans for most of her life. Sometimes they were just for basic things like how to get her Barbie doll out of her faux leather Barbie pants after being left in the sun all day, and others, like the one today, were a bit more serious. But the important thing was that her plan now meant that the situation was under control. That was also another reason why she knew that her dad would be coming back. Because he always had a plan.

"What is it?" Kara squealed.

"It's simple. The reason I don't need to learn how to use my magic is because I'm not going to be a djinn anymore. I'm going to make him turn me back. I mean, we live in the twenty-first century; people can't just go around turning innocent girls in djinns. And if that fails, I can always go to the Djinn Council that he was talking about. I doubt they'd be too happy to hear what he did."

"Oh." Kara didn't look quite as excited as Sophie had expected her to. Instead, her friend chewed her lips for a moment before letting out a cautious cough. "The thing is, Sophie, he might not bother to come back for days. Or weeks even...and it's not that I don't want to paint you every day, because I totally don't mind, it's just, what happens when it rains? Or when you want a shower? Or..." Kara trailed off, and Sophie looked at her friend in alarm, since her plan hadn't taken that fact into account. Suddenly, she felt ill, but before she could say anything Harvey grinned.

"Actually, I've got an idea that might help," he said, and both girls immediately turned to him.

"You do? What is it?" Kara demanded.

"Well." He shrugged as he paused from eating Cheetos. "I know I can't paint skin like Kara can, and I definitely can't try and convince a djinn to change his mind about something like Sophie can, but I sure can research the pants off stuff, so why don't I just do some djinn research? Plus, when this djinn does turn up, it might give Sophie more to bargain with. Don't forget that knowledge is power!"

"Harvey, you're a genius." Kara gave him a spontaneous hug, and Sophie felt a surge of relief go racing through her. Then Kara began to bob her head up and down in excitement. "We can start now. Sophie's mom is working late, and—"

"And aren't you going shopping with your mom this afternoon?" Sophie reminded her friend and then watched as Kara's face fell.

"Oh, man. I totally forgot. She wants some help with Uncle Phil's birthday present, but I never would've agreed if I'd known that Sophie was going to have an orange emergency. Should I tell her that something else has come up?"

"Definitely not." Sophie and Harvey both shook their heads at the same time, since while Kara was laid back, her mom was anything but, and she didn't take kindly to having her plans changed. "Besides," Sophie added, "as soon as we find anything, we'll just send you a text or IM you."

"Are you sure?" Kara still didn't look convinced.

"Of course," Harvey assured her. "Besides, I'll probably get it done faster if you and Sophie aren't both in the same room together, since that's when you normally decide to paint my toenails or braid my hair."

"We only did that once," Sophie protested before ruefully grinning. "But it's a good point. Plus, whenever Kara is around, Meg tends to shadow us."

"Fine," Kara reluctantly agreed before waving goodbye to them both. Once she had gone, Sophie turned to Harvey.

"I've just got to get Meg from next door, but I won't be long."

He nodded, and Sophie quickly made her way to the Daltons' house, where Meg and her (sometimes) best friend Jessica were eating cupcakes and discussing their new teacher. Sophie thanked Mrs. Dalton for picking Meg up, and the sisters made their way back to where Harvey was waiting for them.

Sophie let out an unconscious sigh of relief as soon as she stepped onto the porch of the two-story weatherboard home. She'd been born in this house, and despite the peeling paint and the lawn that had needed mowing for weeks, being here made her feel like everything would be okay again.

"What's wrong with your face?" Meg suddenly demanded as Sophie unlocked the front door, thereby proving that if six-year-old kids really did rule the world, then everyone would be in a lot of a trouble. "And why is Harvey here?"

"There's nothing wrong with my face, and Harvey is helping me with some homework," Sophie said quickly as she tugged Harvey's hoodie down over her brow and went for a change of subject. "Anyway, how was your first day? Your new teacher sounds nice."

"Well, she's not; she's awful, and first grade sucks," Meg retorted in a blunt voice, but before Sophie could reply, her sister went dashing for the mailbox, and Sophie took the opportunity to quickly unlock the door while Meg couldn't see her paint-smeared fingers.

However, the minute she stepped inside there was a yowling noise from over by the window, and Sophie looked up to see Mr. Jaws glaring at her, his black and white fur sticking up and his back arched like the letter *N*.

Harvey looked at him in fascination as he stopped eating Cheetos for a moment. "Wow, will you check out that body language. I'm pretty sure that something is bothering him. I wonder if it's because he can sense what's happened to you. Cats have a sixth sense about these things."

"I don't know, but whatever it is, he needs to stop it," Sophie said in alarm before she turned to the cat. "Shhhh," she hissed in a low voice as Mr. Jaws continued to stare at her as if she'd refused to feed him for ten days (which, for the record, was completely unfair since the longest the cat had gone without food was about a minute). "Seriously, Mr. Jaws, be quiet. Just go and chase your shadow or something."

Yeah, right, the only thing I intend on doing is snarling at you until someone else figures out that you've turned into an orange-skinned freakazoid, the cat seemed to say. But before Sophie could reply Meg came racing into the house carrying a bundle of letters under her arm. Thankfully, she seemed oblivious to the laser beams of hate that Mr. Jaws was putting out, and instead she darted over to the couch and scrambled under it.

Sophie, who had once found her sister asleep in the laundry basket, didn't even blink. Instead, she headed to the kitchen, pleased that Meg was distracted. She grabbed a couple of packets of mini Oreos and hurried back out.

"Meg," she called as she tossed the Oreos onto the coffee table and dumped the library books she'd been lugging around all day. "There's a snack and some books here for you. If you want anything else, you're going to have to get it yourself because I've got some stuff to do in my room, and I don't want to be bugged. Understand me? Oh, and mom doesn't want you watching any shark shows, so it's cartoons or nothing."

"What? But Mr. Jaws hates cartoons. They scare him." Meg appeared out from under the sofa.

"And shark programs don't?" Harvey raised an eyebrow, which Meg rewarded with a frosty look. He held up his hands. "Sorry, of course they don't scare him, because sharks are awesome."

"That's right, they *are* awesome." Meg agreed with a sniff before turning to Sophie. "So please can I watch a shark show," she begged in a high-pitched baby voice that Sophie recognized only too well. It was the kind that usually meant her sister wasn't going to give in, which in turn meant that she would be knocking on the bedroom door all afternoon. *Which definitely wouldn't be a good idea.* Sophie let out a sigh.

"Okay, fine. But if mom finds out, then you're on your own."

However, instead of saying thank you, Meg merely switched on the television and disappeared back under the sofa, making Sophie think that she'd been played. Still, the important thing was that hopefully Meg would now leave them alone. She nodded to Harvey, and they both made their way upstairs.

The minute Sophie got into the familiar yellow-and-white wallpapered room, complete with the heavy cast-iron bed that her dad had almost lost his thumb and sanity trying to set up for her, she shut the door and let out a long breath.

"Okay, so getting past Meg is one hurdle down," she said as Harvey dropped his backpack onto the ground and sat down in front of the computer, his fingers already flying across the keyboard. As he logged on, Sophie hurried over to the mirror that was hanging next to her favorite Eddie Henry poster.

Eddie was the Neanderthal Joe bassist, and despite the fact that most people crushed on the lead singer James Wilton, for Sophie it had always been Eddie (Did she mention that Jonathan Tait actually looked a lot like him?).

She instantly put her hand over Eddie's eyes before using her other hand to push back Harvey's hoodie and properly inspect her paint-smeared face. It was a credit to Kara's artistic skills that Sophie's even looked halfway passable. However, the moment she wiped her cheek with a tissue, Sophie realized that nothing had changed. Part of her felt like crying (a really, really big part); however, she forced herself to bite back her tears.

"I'm a positive person," she quietly reminded herself. "A very, very positive person." And right now she was positive she was orange.

"Hey, are you okay?" Harvey looked up. "You look like you're having a mini freak-out."

"Sorry." Sophie dragged her gaze away from the mirror and realized that she really would've had a mini freak-out if Harvey hadn't been there. "So how's it going? Have you found much stuff?"

"I have," he said as he plugged his memory stick into the USB drive and started to download it. "A lot of it's pretty basic, and there is absolutely no mention of orange skin here, so I'm going through a list of folk stories involving djinns. Sometimes you get more truth from fiction."

"Good idea," she agreed, forcing herself not to look back into the mirror. "And actually, see if you can find the story about the foolish djinn and the foolish girl who rescued him. That's the one my dad used to read to me all the time."

Harvey chewed his lip in concentration as he made his way down the list before shaking his head. "Nope. That one's not here, but I'll try another site, and then I thought I'd—"

However, the rest of his words were cut off by the sound of his cell phone. He quickly pulled it from his pocket and checked the text message, which had just come in. Sophie watched in alarm as his face went pale.

"Hey, is everything okay?"

"What?" He blinked for a moment before he finally looked up and shot her an apologetic smile. "Yeah everything's fine. Well, sort of. That was my mom. She wants me to go home, but I'm just going to tell her that—"

"You're going to do no such thing." She put her hand over his to stop him from texting back a reply (while trying to ignore her own orange, paint-smeared fingers). "I'm sure that the djinn isn't too far away."

"Are you sure?" Harvey didn't look convinced, but Sophie gave an adamant nod of her head as she grabbed his backpack.

"Yes, I promise."

"Okay, but I'll definitely do some more research tonight, and by tomorrow we'll all be djinn experts."

"Thanks, Harvey. You're the best." She grinned at him while secretly crossing her fingers, since tomorrow she planned to forget that djinns even existed. She then waited until Harvey left before she brought her hands crashing together in an almighty clap to try and summon the djinn.

Then she repeated it again and again until it finally built up into an earsplitting crescendo. Yes, her hands hurt like crazy, but as she continued to clap, she didn't care, because—

"You know, you don't need to clap so loudly. I'm right here," a voice said from over to the left, and Sophie felt her eyes widen as she realized the djinn was sitting on her bed. His long legs were crossed at the knees, and his hands were neatly folded in front of him as if he didn't have a care in the world.

"You." Sophie immediately threw Harvey's hood back off her face and marched over to him. "Where have you been? I've been clapping for *hours*."

"Yeah, sorry about that." The djinn shrugged. "I did go

back to that school place of yours, but you seemed a bit hysterical, so I thought I'd give you some time to settle down, since hysterical girls aren't really my forte... *and burning Sahara sands, what have you done to your face?*"

"It's called paint." Sophie gritted her teeth and narrowed her eyes. "Because, in case you're too dumb to realize, humans don't normally walk around 'that school place' looking orange."

"Well, I might not be an expert on humans like you are, but all the same, I'm fairly certain that they don't normally walk around covered in paint, either," the djinn countered, which only caused Sophie to glare at him some more.

"Trust me, I don't intend to anymore. Now that you're here, can you please swap me back to normal?" As she spoke she nodded her head to positively reinforce her message (which Harvey had actually taught her from his body language book. So far it had worked three times on her mom and once on Mr. Jaws, so Sophie felt confident using it now).

"What little part of our previous conversation did you not understand?" The djinn got to his feet, wandered over to Sophie's bookshelf, and started to examine one of her ancient Tamagotchi virtual pets. "There is no swapping back. You're a djinn. Whether you like it or not."

"But I can't be," Sophie explained to him patiently as she continued to nod her head. "Look, I don't who you are, but—"

"Malik."

"What?" Sophie stared at him as he gave the Tamagotchi a curious sniff.

"Malik. That's my name. Not that I would normally tell you that, since rule number one for any djinn is to never let anyone find out what your true name is. By the way, you should actually write that rule down. Anyway, I guess now that I'm dead it doesn't matter. Malik, Malik, Malik. Wow, you have no idea how great it feels to say that," Malik marveled.

"Well, *Malik, Malik, Malik,* I'm pleased that you're so happy, but if you can't understand why you need to turn me back to normal, then perhaps you should take me to this Djinn Council of yours, because I'm sure that they would be most interested to hear what you've been up to."

Malik instantly burst out laughing, and it took several minutes for him to finally stop. "Sorry," he eventually apologized as he wiped his eyes. "But it's been a long time since I've heard anything quite so funny."

"And why exactly is it so funny?" Sophie demanded, folding her arms in front of her.

"You thinking that the Djinn Council might give two hoots about you." Malik was still silently shaking. Sophie gulped, since until that minute she had herself convinced. Then she remembered that the djinn was a self-confessed liar.

"And why should I believe you?" She narrowed her eyes.

"Absolutely no reason at all." He didn't look remotely bothered as he gave her a casual shrug. "But it doesn't make it any less true. So you can either forget about this idea that there's a get-out clause, or you can make yourself miserable for the next couple of thousand years. It really is your call."

"But I can't be a djinn," Sophie persisted, while trying to ignore the desperate edge to her voice. So much for her fabulous new plan.

"You know since you still seem to have a problem accepting this thing, how about I just give you some alone time, and then when you're ready to talk about it, you can clap your hands?"

"What?" Sophie blinked at him before giving a resolute shake of her head. "I'm not falling for that one again. You can stay here until this thing is sorted out."

"But there's nothing to sort out," Malik reminded her. "You're a djinn, and if you want to keep doing the 'argh, but it can't be happening to me' thing, then that's fine, but I'd rather not be here to witness it."

"But—"

"Aha. See, there you go again." Malik pointed his finger at her. "Look, let me spell it out for you. Under that paint, your skin is now the color of a gorgeous tropical sunset. There's a buzzing noise in your ears that indicates that you're tuning in to your new powers. And finally, your core body temperature has risen by about five degrees as you become a true child of the smokeless flame.

And you know what all of that stuff means?"

"T-that I'm coming down with the flu?" Sophie asked hopefully as she rubbed her ears and tried not to think about her burning cheeks and orange skin.

"That you're a djinn," Malik corrected.

"So what are you saying? That I really am stuck like this for the rest of my life?" Sophie felt her lips start to wobble as the reality started to hit her. The worst thing was that she didn't even need Malik to confirm what she already knew. After all, a girl could ignore the fact that her skin was orange for only so long. Or that she was boiling hot despite the San Diego fall weather, or even that her ears were still buzzing like she'd just spent the entire night in the mosh pit of a Neanderthal Joe concert. Something was definitely happening to her, and from the sounds of it, that something was the fact that she had turned into a djinn.

Sophie dropped her head into her hands and resisted the urge to scream. This surely had to be the worst first day back at school. Ever.

"YOU KNOW I DON'T MEAN TO INTERRUPT WHEN YOU are quite clearly having a moment." Malik gave a polite cough about ten minutes later. "But you've been quiet for a while now, and the thing is, I'm getting a bit hungry. I don't suppose you have anything to eat around here? Now that I don't have any powers, I guess I'll just have to start getting my food the old-fashioned way."

Sophie, who was just in the middle of having an official freak-out (about the size of a small European country), finally felt herself snap out of it as she looked up at Malik in disbelief.

"Okay, so let me just be clear about this. You've come along and *completely* ruined my life, and now you're asking for food?"

"Hey, it's been a really tough day," Malik protested before seeming to notice the dark look Sophie was throwing him. He suddenly shrugged. "But I'm just a ghost, so who needs food, right? And I know I opted out of the whole eternal-life thing, but honestly, it's not so bad."

"Yeah, right," Sophie started to mutter before an idea suddenly occurred to her. "Oh, that's it! You tricked me into wearing the ring, so why don't I just trick someone else into wearing it? Not anyone I know, of course, but perhaps a bad person?"

"Yes, why not give unlimited power to an evil person. That's a great idea," Malik said before shaking his head. "And I hate to dry out your oasis, but you would have to have lived for about a thousand years before you would be even close to having the power to convince someone to take the ring off you. And then there's the whole thing about it potentially killing them. Trust me when I tell you that it's not as easy as it looks. By the way, what's that pinging noise?"

"Oh." Sophie looked over to her computer. She was supposed to turn it off when she went to school to save electricity, but she had obviously forgotten. "It's probably just one of my friends IMing me to see if I'm still orange."

"IMing?" Malik walked over to the keyboard and gave it a curious poke with his finger, but Sophie ignored him as she tried to stay cool. Of course it wasn't easy when (a) she was actually boiling hot, and (b) she was apparently a djinn forever after. Even worse, a quick glance at the clock told her that her mom would be home soon, which meant that her new plan had to involve getting her skin color sorted out as quickly as possible.

"Malik," she said as he picked up the computer mouse and started to lick it. "Malik," she repeated in a louder voice, but when he still didn't answer, she was forced to march over and take the mouse out of his hands. "Malik, will you please concentrate."

"Sorry," he apologized as he continued to stare at the mouse much like it was a piece of chocolate cake. "What did you want?"

"I want to know how to lose the orange skin."

"You don't like being orange?" He lifted an eyebrow in surprise.

"Not even a little bit," Sophie assured him. "So can you please zap it away?"

"Sorry, I thought I explained that now I'm dead, I don't have any magic at all. Just the ability to walk through walls, which between you and me is pretty cool. Oh, and this—" he suddenly added as he clicked his fingers and she found herself staring at someone who looked a whole lot like Zac Efron.

Sophie's jaw dropped as Zac gave her a half smile.

"Neat, isn't it?" Malik's voice came out of Zac's mouth. "I had no idea that ghosts could still shape-shift. Anyway, I was thinking since you're young that you might feel more comfortable with someone a bit closer to your own age, so I took the liberty of looking through some magazines. It was either this guy or someone called Jonas Brother."

Sophie dropped down to her bed and rubbed her brow, while reminding herself that she was a very positive person, and just because it appeared as if her djinn guide had not only ruined her life but obviously was insane as well, that was no reason for her to freak out. She just needed to take a deep breath and think happy thoughts.

Ah. That was better. After another calming lungful of oxygen she looked up to where Malik/Zac was inspecting his fingers with interest. She plastered on a bright smile.

"Okay, so I suppose you'll need to teach me how to do it. After all, didn't you tell me that it's your job to help me deal with all of this?"

"You want to learn how to do a double helix spell on your first day?" he double-checked before shaking his head. "Sorry, but that just ain't going to happen. In fact, until your ring has been properly cleansed, you won't be able to do any magic at all. Even when you can do magic it takes quite a while for you to learn how to control it all. Thankfully, now that you're immortal you have all the time in the world."

"But there must be something I can do?" Sophie pleaded while secretly wondering if she was going to be sick.

"Well, there is Rufus the Furious." Malik paused and rubbed his Zac-like chin for a moment. "He came up with a potion that completely takes it away. Of course, at the time we all laughed at him, since who in their right mind would want to change from orange to a rancid flesh color? But as it turns out, loads of djinns wanted to, which is why Rufus the Furious is now known as Rufus the Filthy Rich, and—"

"So there is something I can use to make me look like normal again?" Sophie widened her eyes as she felt a surge of relief go racing through her. Thank goodness for positive thinking.

"Yes, that's what I just said." Malik looked confused. "So does that mean you want some?"

"Absolutely, with bells on top," Sophie assured him as she pulled Harvey's hoodie back over her forehead. "First I just need to drop Meg back around to the Daltons' place. How long should I tell Mrs. Dalton that we'll be gone?"

"It shouldn't take too long." Malik gave a dismissive shrug. "Probably four days. Five tops, though it will depend on the trade winds. They can be a bit funny this time of year. Of course it would easier if you could use your magic, but—"

"Four or five days?" Sophie instantly threw the hoodie back from her head and used her hands to fan down her burning face. "Where exactly is this place?"

"Istanbul."

"Istanbul?" Sophie repeated just in case she had made a mistake. Unlike Kara, who excelled at art, and Harvey, who, despite his appearance, excelled in everything math and science related, Sophie's best subject was history, and her second-best subject was geography, which meant she knew exactly where Istanbul was (or, more to the point, exactly where it wasn't—i.e., down the street).

"That's correct. Why are you looking at me like that? Is something wrong?"

"I'm looking at you like this because I'm eleven years old," Sophie replied as she continued to fan her boiling face. "I can't even go to the mall on my own, so Istanbul is sort of out of the question."

"Huh. So that I did not know." Malik rubbed his chin for a minute before shrugging. "Oh, well, I guess you'll just have to get used to the orange then. Besides, you'd be surprised at how many colors it actually goes with. I mean, you've got all your reds and yellows, and then it contrasts nicely with green and—"

"Stop!" She commanded while trying not to freak out about the fact that not only was she an orange djinn but that the ghost who was meant to be guiding her was quite clearly insane. "You're not helping here. There has to be something."

"Let's see, double helix or a visit to Rufus to get his potion." Malik ticked off his fingers before looking back up and shaking his head. "Nope. Sorry, those are the only two options... and there's that weird pinging noise again. Are you sure there isn't anything trapped in there, because I once fought this ghul that made a very similar noise. Nasty creature it was. In fact, in the end the only way I could stop it was by chopping off its head. Actually, you should make a note of that. Ghuls respond best to head chopping. Very important."

"I've got no idea what a ghul is, but I can promise you that there's nothing in there but wires and stuff," Sophie assured him as she once again glanced over to see that both Harvey and Kara were now impatiently nudging her online. "Now come on, Malik, if you're my guide, then you need to figure something out."

"But I still don't understand what it does?" Malik, who didn't seem remotely bothered by Sophie's panic, was instead tentatively poking the screen, much like one would poke a sleeping tiger. Sophie gritted her teeth.

"It's a computer, and most people use it for the Internet, which is a place where you can go and look up just about anything. I mean, Harvey even found loads of stuff on—"

However, the rest of the words died on her lips as she realized how dumb she had been. Of course. It was so simple that she couldn't quite believe that she hadn't thought of it sooner.

"What are you doing?" Malik demanded as Sophie edged him out of the way and brought up a search engine. Then she grinned in delight as she studied the results.

"If I can't go to Istanbul, I'm going to see if Istanbul can come to me."

"Well, I don't mean to discourage you, but when Solomon attempted to get one of his djinns to move Israel a bit closer to France (apparently he had a thing for croissants), the whole exercise was a total fail from start to finish."

"I'm not talking about magic." Sophie shook her head as she clicked on a link. "I'm talking about Google... ta-da."

"Yes, but," Malik started to say before he leaned forward and once again pointed to the screen, this time in astonishment. "Hey, that's him. That's Rufus. Ooooh, though you know, he really shouldn't let people see his left profile like that. It's not what I would call flattering. Anyway, what is this thing he's in?"

"It's called a Web site, and thankfully this one has online shopping," Sophie explained as she quickly scanned the first page.

Welcome to Rufus's Bazaar, where we hope to cater to all of your djinn needs, from turbo-charged rugs to sahir repellents. All major credit cards are accepted, and on occasion we do trade in livestock as well, but only if they're house trained and don't swear...

"Interesting." Malik looked impressed as Sophie started to scroll through the products before realizing she didn't have a clue what she was looking for.

"So what's this stuff called?"

"He called it Rufus's Glorious and World-Famous Orange-Detractor Potion," the djinn told her before rolling his eyes. "Which between you and me is a slightly egotistical name, but then that's Rufus all over. Two parts sand and eight parts high opinion of himself. Oh, there it is." He suddenly pointed to a small icon that had a circle-shaped bottle on it.

Sophie immediately clicked on it. A larger image of the bottle immediately sprang up on the screen along with a description in which Rufus solemnly assured his faithful shoppers that this potion would take the user back to whatever his or her natural skin color had been, all for the one low price of two hundred dollars.

"Two hundred dollars?" Sophie widened her eyes before turning to Malik. "That's a lot of money. Besides, if this Rufus is a djinn *and* a friend of yours, couldn't we just ask him to do the double helix spell on me. As a favor?"

Malik pushed back his caramel-colored Zac Efron hair as if to study her better. "Okay, so first thing, I wouldn't exactly call Rufus a friend. Especially after what happened in Egypt, not that I'm allowed to talk about it due to legal reasons. But more importantly, rule number one about being a djinn is that you should never ask another djinn to do you a favor, because you can guarantee that they will want to collect on that favor when it least suits you. Actually, you should write that down. Oh, and while you're at it, you should never borrow money from a djinn either, because they will kill you with the interest rates."

"Why don't I just write down that I should never trust anything a djinn says or does since they are all apparently liars and cheats," Sophie retorted.

"That actually sums it up pretty well," Malik instantly agreed, not looking remotely ashamed about it. "You know, for a kid, you really have a good way with words."

Sophie glared at him for a moment before realizing that it would be completely useless to keep arguing with him. Instead, she let out a reluctant sigh and transferred the potion into her shopping basket.

"Oh, and you might as well get some of that Fruits of the Desert Ring Cleanser as well." Malik pointed to another thing on the screen. "You can probably buy it locally, but Rufus puts a lovely hint of vanilla in this one, which makes it smell pretty."

At thirty dollars a bottle it had better smell pretty, Sophie privately thought as she obediently added it to the basket. Then, when Malik seemed to be done with making her buy stuff, she went to the payment screen.

Technically, she wasn't supposed to do any online shopping, but then again, technically she probably wasn't supposed to be a djinn either, so she figured that the two of them canceled each other out. Besides, she had no intention of her mom finding out about either thing. So instead she went and got her bank details. Her dad, before he disappeared, had been an accountant, and so he had insisted that Sophie start her own junior-saver account when she was three years old.

Then she realized that now wasn't such a great time to be thinking about her dad or her old, normal life, so she concentrated on making sure she didn't muddle the numbers up as she put them in. As she did so, Malik studied the screen with interest.

"So these digits that you're putting into this machine will let you buy stuff?" he wanted to know, and Sophie nodded.

"That's right. But only if you have enough money in

your bank account." Then she frowned for a moment. "Which delivery do I want? Phoenix or Pigeon?"

"Pigeon," Malik instantly replied. "Unless of course you like to be kept waiting for months while the most arrogant, vain, thick-as-a-plank-of-wood bird in existence lies around in the sun, moaning about what a tough life it has just because it got caught in one measly fire, instead of delivering your mail in a timely fashion."

Sophie blinked. "Er, okay, so pigeon it is. By the way, how long will it take?" she asked as she hit Enter and completed the order. However, before Malik could even reply there was rustling of feathers and a pink bird that didn't look like any sort of pigeon Sophie had ever seen suddenly appeared on the corner of her computer desk with a large parcel in its beak. It squawked twice, and dropped the parcel in her lap, and then studied her expectantly from its wide violet eyes.

"Are you kidding me with this?" Sophie stared at the package, then the bird, and finally at Malik.

"Kidding you? I don't understand what you mean. Isn't this what you wanted?" Malik looked confused.

"Yes, it's what I wanted, but I didn't realize it would be quite so fast. I mean, that's just crazy," she explained before she realized that the pink bird was not only still staring at her, but she was fairly sure it hadn't even blinked either. Creepy, much? She suddenly remembered that Harvey had once told her about a horror movie involving killer birds, and she shifted uncomfortably in her seat.

"Er, Malik, why is it looking at me like that?"

"I think it's waiting for a tip."

"A tip?" Sophie winced as she thought of her empty money box (thanks, cute belt to match jeans) and her equally empty bank account (thanks, potion and creepy pink pigeon delivery service). "As in money?"

"I guess it could eat money at a push, but worms would probably be better." Malik shrugged as he reached forward and ruffled the bird's feathers. The pigeon quickly pecked at his hand, while still not breaking eye contact with Sophie.

"Oh." Sophie nodded while trying to ignore the fact that her life was getting more surreal by the moment. She carefully put the parcel on the table and glanced around before catching sight of Harvey's Cheetos. She paused and wrinkled her nose in confusion since Harvey never normally left any food behind. Then she dismissed it because the main thing was that she now had some food. She held up the bag to Malik. "Well, these aren't worms, but perhaps they would be okay?"

"I don't know? What are they?" he asked, and Sophie looked at him in surprise. It was one thing not to know about the Internet, but to not know about Cheetos?

"They're like a cheesy snack food," she explained as she held out the packet to him. He took a couple, and she was just about to offer one to the bird when Malik whipped the bag out of her hand and turned to the pigeon and started to speak to it in some rapid-fire language that she'd never heard of before. And along with the talking, there was a lot of arm gesturing on Malik's behalf.

For a moment the bird spread its wings and started to flap them in Malik's face, but instead of looking scared, Malik continued the conversation in an animated (and very loud) fashion before the bird finally disappeared from sight in a flutter, leaving behind a single pink feather.

"What was that about?" Sophie blinked in alarm. "I hope I didn't offend it by offering it a Cheeto?"

"Offend it?" Malik snorted as he hugged the packet close to his chest. "Who cares if you offended it? It's just a stupid bird, and besides, there was no way I was going to let you waste these perfect little twisty sticks of delicious orange goodness on that dirty creature. And so I told it."

"But what about the tip? You said I needed to give it one," Sophie reminded him as she watched Malik shovel Cheetos into his mouth. She didn't even know ghosts could eat food, but right now that was the least of her worries.

"Don't worry, I gave it a good tip. I told it to never put a red shirt in with a white wash." Malik gave a dismissive shrug. "Anyway, who cares about the bird? Tell me more about these divine morsels? Did humans really invent them? I think I've been underrating mankind."

"Okay, so perhaps when things are less crazy we can have a long discussion on the history of Cheetos, but right now I need to use this potion." Sophie caught sight of the box that was still sitting on the corner of the desk. It didn't take her long to open it up and lift out a small, bright red oval-shaped bottle that looked more like something Britney Spears would release as a perfume than something designed to change your skin color. On one side was a small picture of Rufus the Furious, and on the other side it simply said to take half a capful once a day. Well, that sounded simple enough, and she carefully poured out the liquid that ended up being as red as the bottle. Perhaps that meant it would taste like strawberries?

She took a tentative sip and pulled a face. Okay, so cancel the strawberry thing. It tasted more like old shoes and stinky socks. However, she forced herself to finish it off and then looked down at her arm.

It was no longer orange.

Like seriously.

"It worked." She raced over to the mirror and stared at her face. Yes, the scattering of freckles was still there, not to mention the small bump on her nose, but the main thing was that she no longer looked like a special-edition orange M&M. "It really, really worked."

"Well, duh." Malik rolled his eyes as he sat down on her bed and started to flick through an old copy of *Seventeen* that Kara had left behind. "Didn't I say that being a djinn wasn't so bad, but you were all *'No, I'm eleven'* and *'Argh, my life is over'* when really you were making a big deal about nothing."

"Well, I must admit that I'm feeling a bit more positive now that the orange is gone," Sophie confessed as she continued to inspect her face.

"There you go." Malik nodded supportively as he held the magazine closer to his face to get a better look at something. "And even better, you didn't get any spots or horns, which, if you ask me, is a real bonus."

"What?" Sophie yelped as she immediately started to check her head for horns. "There are side effects? No one said anything about side effects."

"I wouldn't call it them side effects, more like little tricks that Rufus sometimes likes to play. Before he was Rufus the Furious, he was actually Rufus the Crazy." Malik gave a dismissive wave as he put the magazine away. "Anyway, the important thing is that it didn't affect you that way."

"And he thinks that's funny?" Sophie, who was finally convinced there were no horns, stopped patting her head. However, before she could say anything else, she heard the familiar rattle of a ten-year-old Toyota pulling into the driveway. She turned to Malik in panic. "My mom's home. What should I do?"

"Er, I would assume that you should do what you always do. Complain about homework, refuse to eat your Brussels sprouts, and moan about how early you have to go to bed. Why? What did you have in mind?"

"I mean about the djinn thing?" Sophie gritted her teeth as she fanned her face to try to cool down. "Is there anything special I should do to hide it from her? I mean, it's one thing to trick my teachers, but my mom never misses anything."

"Oh, I see what you're saying. You're worried that you might suddenly start to levitate up in the air or turn your younger sister into a tow truck. Is that it?"

"Well, I wasn't before, but I am now." Sophie gulped. "So could that happen?"

"Of course not. You're a djinn, not a psychopathic nutcase." Malik rolled his eyes. "See, this is what I'm talking about. You really need to stop thinking that your life is going to be so different. Honestly, being a djinn is the most normal thing in the world, and most of the time you won't even notice it. So why don't you go downstairs and just act like you always do. And actually, while you're down there, I don't suppose you could rustle up any more of those Cheetos? Oh, and some chocolate-covered ants if you've got any. I love those things..."

For a moment Sophie paused before she realized that what he was saying made total sense. Okay, not the part about the chocolate-covered ants because, ewh. But everything else was right. How had she not realized sooner that she was overreacting? Besides, she was a positive person, and positive people didn't dwell on the negative (or the orange) stuff, they focused on the good things. And with that thought in mind, she took a deep breath and walked downstairs.

10

STOP LOOKING AT ME LIKE THAT," SOPHIE COMmanded the following morning as she and her two friends sat on top of one of the decorative boulders that dotted the entrance to Robert Robertson Middle School.

"Sorry." Kara flushed as she let go of Sophie's arm, which she had been inspecting. "But I just can't get over the fact that you really are a djinn."

"And that you're not orange anymore," Harvey added as he let go of Sophie's other arm. "What are the chances of it coming back?"

"Apparently none, as long as I take the potion stuff each day. Though when Malik teaches me how to do a double helix spell, then I won't even need to do that," Sophie said patiently, since her friends weren't the only ones who were struggling to come to terms with it all. Though perhaps the weirdest thing was how normal everything still seemed.

In fact, despite all of Malik's assurances (and continued pleas for food) when Sophie had gone downstairs yesterday afternoon, she had fully expected some sort of Armageddon to happen. Instead, it had ended up being just like every other night in their house. Her mom had burned the dinner, complained about what a rotten day she'd had at work, and then said she was going to do some pottery before really falling asleep while watching *Friends* reruns. Then at breakfast, Meg had indulged in another Oscar-winning "I don't want to go to school" tantrum.

Though, actually, Sophie hadn't minded that so much, since it kept their mom from attempting to have an "important talk" with them. Especially since her "important talks" normally involved new and normally painful ways of saving money, and this time she had the funny feeling that it might include getting rid of broadband. And while Sophie could (vaguely) live with the fact she didn't have a cell phone, there was no way she could cope if she was disconnected.

Still, the main thing was that the only one who had acted like there was something strange going on was Mr. Jaws, but since he tended to get weirded out by the sight of a paper bag, no one really paid much attention to him.

"So what about magic?" Kara demanded, an excited gleam in her eye. "When do you start doing some?"

Sophie shook her head. "He didn't mention any of that. He just went on and on about how important it was for me to cleanse my djinn ring every day for a week before I could even begin to access my powers. In fact, I do believe his exact words were: 'It would be like me trying to teach you how to drive a submarine using only a rubber band and a bird's feather,'" she said, mimicking Malik's voice.

"That's the weirdest analogy that I've ever heard in my life." Harvey scratched his head as he started to flick through the reams of paper that were sitting on his lap. He hadn't been joking when he had promised to do some more research last night—Sophie was sure he'd used half a tree just to print everything out. He finally retrieved a particular page and held it up. "But I think I know what he means. According to everything I've read about magic, there is a real cause-and-effect thing going on, which means that magic shouldn't be used lightly."

"Are you sure?" Kara sounded disappointed.

"I'm sure," he said as he waved the paper at her. "It also says here that djinns are neither good nor bad, which is a relief since we now know that Sophie won't be going all Dark Side on us. Oh, and by the way, I couldn't find any reference to that story you were telling me about the foolish djinn. Are you sure you remembered it right?"

"Definitely." Sophie nodded her head. "I swear I heard it a zillion times." But before she could say anything else Harvey's cell phone started to beep. A second later Kara's did as well, and as they both dug them out of their pockets to study the screens, Sophie noticed that all around them, the other students were doing the same thing.

"What is it?" she demanded, but instead of answering her, her two friends exchanged a concerned look with each other, and Sophie felt her heart start to sink. Even though

Robert Robertson Middle School didn't have their own *Gossip Girl* ninja who could spread bad news at the touch of a Send button, she suddenly had an awful feeling that the text messages somehow involved her.

"Nothing," Kara and Harvey both said a little bit too quickly, which only confirmed Sophie's suspicions.

"Come on, guys, you can tell me the worst." She gulped. "Did someone see what happened yesterday and they've spread it around the school? Because of course it will ruin my life, but I can take it. Honestly, I—"

"Soph, it's not that at all." Kara reached out and squeezed her hand.

"So why are you both looking like that? The last time you did that, it was when you didn't want to tell me that I didn't get the lead part in the school musical."

"Yeah, well, it's never nice to tell someone that she can't sing," Harvey said before Kara glared at him. "Er, not that this is anything to do with that. The thing is, we just received the location text for where the Neanderthal Joe tickets are going to go on sale, but we didn't want to tell you because we know you had to spend all your money on your anti-orange potion."

"Where is it?" Sophie tried to hide her jealousy. To think that yesterday she was orange and today she was about to turn green.

"In town, right next to my mom's work," Kara admitted.

"Oh." Sophie gulped. "Well, that's good. It means you won't miss out."

"But the thing is, Soph, we're not going to go to the concert either," Kara said, the words tumbling out of her mouth in a rush.

"What?" Sophie stared at them both as they hurried in through the main entrance to their homeroom. "You guys have to go. You've been dying to go for, like, ever, and now that we know where the tickets are going to be sold..."

"We're not changing our minds," Harvey said in an unusually firm voice as they reached the room just seconds before their teacher. "We both discussed it, and it just wouldn't be the same without you."

"I can't believe you guys would do that for me." Sophie sniffed.

"Well, you'd better believe it. Besides, there is this body-language book that I've been after, and now I'll totally be able to afford it," Harvey said with a grin.

"And I can buy a new easel," Kara added just as Mr. Collins came in and shot everyone a stern look as if to let them know that chitchat might be okay in fifth grade, but now that they were in sixth grade, things were going to be different.

By lunchtime Sophie realized just how right Mr. Collins was, since for a start in fifth grade there was no such thing as a double math period, but now? Her whole schedule seemed to be littered with the horrible things, and while it was all right for Harvey, who loved math, for Sophie it just made her head hurt. And now she had to double that.

Still, at least that class was over for the day, and she

quickly shoved her math books into her locker and was just about to head to the cafeteria when she heard a coughing noise from behind her.

Sophie's heart froze.

The last time someone had coughed behind her, it was Malik, to inform her that she was a djinn. And despite the fact that she had specifically told him that he couldn't come to her school unless she summoned him, she didn't exactly trust him to obey her. She bit into her bottom lip and slowly turned around.

However, instead of seeing a ghostly djinn with Cheetos smeared all over his face, she discovered that the person standing behind her was actually Jonathan Tait.

Oh God. It was Jonathan Tait!

Sophie felt her jaw go slack, and for a moment she just stared at him before discreetly checking if there was someone else behind her. However, that section of the corridor was empty as kids continued to move in a steady stream toward the cafeteria, and so she turned back around to face him while trying not to lament the fact that she had spent practically her whole vacation choosing yesterday's outfit and about half a nanosecond choosing the one she had on today.

"Hey, you don't have a pen I can borrow, do you?" he asked (in actual words—directed at her!).

"What?" she asked in a blank voice as she tried and failed not to marvel at how gorgeous he was. He should always wear blue T-shirts because they totally brought out the blue in his eyes. In fact, if she was the president of the Universe, she would make that a new law.

"Pen? I just need to write something down," he elaborated, and Sophie willed herself to stop acting like a stupid idiot.

"Right, pen. Yes. I have one of those. Definitely." She reached into her bag and frantically felt around for her pencil case while trying to ignore that her cheeks felt even hotter than normal. Finally, her fingers curled around the case and she pulled it out in triumph. "Ta-da."

"Er, thanks." Jonathan seemed to be biting back a smile as he grabbed a pen from her and quickly wrote something down on the back of his hand. It looked like "must buy spider," but since Sophie was looking at it upside down, she could be wrong about that (she certainly hoped so because there was nothing good about spiders).

"No problem at all." Sophie tried to push the image of spiders from her mind. "Whenever you need a pen, I'm your girl. Oh, yes, I am."

"O-kay," he said in a casual voice as he handed the pen back. Then he suddenly peered carefully at her face. "Hey, don't I know you from somewhere?"

"I-I was a year behind you at Miller Road Elementary," Sophie admitted, and he nodded his head.

"Oh, yeah. That's it. Sophie Campbell. I remember you now," he continued as he threaded his thumbs through the loops of his jeans and grinned at her. What did that mean? Did that mean he liked her? Sophie made a mental note to ask Harvey if his book made any reference to thumbs in jeans loops. "By the way, I like your T-shirt. They rock it so hard."

"What?" Sophie said, before nervously looking down to see what T-shirt she was wearing. Please don't let it be her ancient Mickey Mouse one that she used to think was retro but was probably just juvenile. Thankfully, instead of mouse ears, she realized she was wearing her favorite Neanderthal Joe T-shirt. *Oh, Universe, I owe you. Big time.* The Joes hadn't come to San Diego on their last tour, but her mom's friend in Los Angeles had gone to the concert and bought Sophie a tour T-shirt, which was pretty much the coolest thing in the whole wide world. *Apart, obviously, from this very moment.*

"I know, right. I love them. Especially 'Zombie Vegas.' That song blows my mind." She grinned at him, while secretly pleased that she had rediscovered the power of speech.

"A bonus-track girl. I'm impressed." Jonathan grinned back at her, and Sophie felt a stab of perfect happiness go racing through her. She and Jonathan Tait were talking. In a real conversation. About Neanderthal Joe. It seriously didn't get any better than that. Actually, it did, and for the next five minutes they stood there debating the merits of downloading singles as opposed to buying the complete album (they were both in favor of the complete album, because nothing could beat owning the original artwork).

"So are you going to see them in concert?" Jonathan suddenly asked.

"Oh." Some of Sophie's happiness seeped away as her shoulders slumped. "It's sort of complicated. I mean, I was going to, but then this other thing came up, and now, well, I'm not quite so sure, though I'm really hoping," she rambled, before realizing that she was making no sense at all. "H-how about you?"

"I'm so there." He held up his hand, and she realized that he hadn't been writing about spiders, he had actually been writing down the location details of where to buy the tickets tomorrow. "My older brother, Finn, said he'd take me so that I could see the Joes without any olds around. Hey, if you do end up going, perhaps you and your friends could come with us? My parents would totally talk to your folks about it and vouch for Finn. Then we could hang out together."

What?

However, before she could reply, a bunch of seventh-grade boys came racing toward Jonathan and started doing some complicated handshakes with him before dragging him off in the other direction. Jonathan did a goofy little shrug of his shoulders and shot her an apologetic look before heading off down the corridor with his friends, leaving Sophie to try to pick her jaw up off the ground. It looked like Malik was wrong, because her life didn't seem like it was going to be the same as normal, it seemed like it was going to be better. And that was something she could definitely live with.

11

WHERE HAVE YOU BEEN?" KARA DEMANDED SEVERal minutes later as she tapped her watch and pushed away the salad she had been eating. "I've been freaking out, worrying that something weird had happened. Why are you smiling like that?"

"I'm not smiling." Sophie smiled. "But seriously, I've just had the most surreal conversation in the whole wide world. Ever. With bells on top."

"More surreal than being told by a ghost that you're now a djinn?" Harvey stopped shoveling a hot dog into his mouth for a moment and lifted a surprised eyebrow.

"Okay, so perhaps that was pretty surreal as well," Sophie was forced to concede before smiling some more. "But trust me, this is up there."

"What?" Kara's eyes were so wide that Sophie was pretty sure they might burst any moment. "You're killing me here. Tell me what happened."

"Okay, so you're never going to believe this, but Jonathan Tait came up to my locker and started talking to me. In real words and everything."

"What?" Kara, who had been doodling on a napkin, snapped the end of her pencil as she looked at Sophie in excitement. "Details. I need details."

"Gladly." Sophie grinned while Harvey made a choking noise on his hot dog. The two girls ignored him as Sophie recounted the entire conversation, complete with hand actions and facial expressions. Once she had finished, she wrinkled her nose. "So what do you think it means?"

"That he has no friends his own age," Harvey piped up.

"Of course he does. Everyone loves Jonathan," Kara corrected before grinning at Sophie. "It's obvious what it means. He was asking you to be his date at the concert."

"Do you really think?" Sophie started to fan her face. She wasn't sure if it was because of the djinn thing or the fact that Jonathan Tait had possibly asked her out.

"I do." Kara nodded, and her long dark hair bounced. "I mean, why else would he offer for us to go with him and his brother? It's just so wonderful. I mean, I know that my mom said she would take us, but seriously we've all seen how edgy she gets when she hits the checkout line at Walmart. Going with Jonathan's brother Finn will be like a zillion times better."

"Apart from the fact that Sophie isn't going to the concert," Harvey reminded them, and Sophie felt her good mood drop. "Besides, not meaning to act like a killjoy here, but considering what happened yesterday, don't you have other things to worry about besides a dumb crush?"

"It's not a dumb crush," Kara retorted in an angry voice before Sophie even had a chance to reply. "And Malik said that there was no reason why she can't lead a normal life, and what could be more normal than this?"

"Okay, fine." Harvey held up his arms in surrender. "It's just, what's the point of dating anyway? I mean, you might get on to begin with, but it's not like it's going to last. I saw a photo of my folks when they were sixteen and all in love. Now when they're in the same room together, it's like they want to gouge each other's eyes out. And I don't need a body-language book to tell me that eye gouging is bad."

"Oh, man, that sucks," Sophie immediately said, suddenly remembering the text message he received yesterday afternoon. And even more alarming, the fact that he hadn't finish his Cheetos. "Harvey, has something else happened?"

"Yeah." He nodded his head so that his straight hair fell into his eyes. "The reason they wanted me to come home yesterday was to tell me that my dad's looking for a place to stay. He's definitely moving out."

"I'm so sorry, H. Why didn't you say anything this morning?" Kara instantly flushed as she reached out and squeezed his hand.

"Well, there was the whole Sophie turning orange and becoming a djinn thing." He shrugged before looking up and letting out a reluctant sigh. "Besides, it's been coming for ages, so I shouldn't really be so surprised. But I didn't mean to bum out Sophie. Especially since Jonathan really isn't that bad—"

"Don't worry about it." Sophie waved aside his apology, but before she could say anything else, a shiver went up her spine and the space around her seemed to go cold. Finally, someone spoke in a low voice.

"Ah, so there you are. I was wondering when I would find you."

Sophie didn't even bother to look up as she realized that, thanks to all the distractions going on around her, she had completely forgotten about the worst problem of them all.

Melissa You-Owe-Me-Two-Hundred-Bucks Tait.

Sophie gulped as she scrambled to her feet and tried not to notice that her face was feeling even hotter than normal. So far no one at school had even mentioned the jeans incident, but Sophie didn't kid herself that it was because Melissa was too kind to tell anyone about it, but rather because the seventh grader liked to play with her victims before she destroyed them. In other words, when she found out that Sophie didn't have any money, she was going to be dead meat.

"So?" Melissa arched one of her eyebrows (an eyebrow that seemed more perfect than it had yesterday. How was that even possible?). "I can see that you've gone back to wearing your regular jeans."

"Oh." Sophie felt her face flush as she glanced down. While the Universe might've been kind enough to guide her into throwing on her favorite Neanderthal Joe T-shirt this morning, it hadn't been quite so considerate about her bottom half, and after deciding that she couldn't wear the jeans again, she had randomly put on the first pair she found. Complete with pink zigzags stitched around the bottom of the leg.

"So anyway, as much fun as it to stand here and chat to a bunch of boring sixth graders, I really have a lot of things to do, so if you could just give me my money, then I'll be on my way," Melissa said as she inspected her nails. They weren't supposed to wear polish to school, but even Sophie, who was a makeup novice, could tell by the shine that Melissa's nails weren't natural. All of which was beside the point, since the only thing that really mattered was that Sophie had spent her entire life savings to buy some anti-orange potion from a djinn called Rufus the Furious yesterday afternoon.

Somehow she didn't think Melissa would be delighted when she found out.

"Okay, so the thing is—" Sophie started to say, but before she could finish, Melissa stopped inspecting her nails and instead moved her hand terrifyingly close to Sophie's nose.

"No. You see I don't do *things*. *Things* are boring. In

fact, *you're* boring, so just give me my money or a brand-new pair of jeans so we can stop having this conversation."

"I wish I could give you the money or a new pair of jeans. In fact, there's nothing that I'd like more," Sophie assured her. "But what I was trying to say—"

"Okay, so perhaps I'm not being clear here?" Melissa fluttered her lashes in a dangerous manner. "Either give me what you owe me, or else. You've got until ten. One. Two. Three—"

Sophie felt her head start to spin as the entire cafeteria seemed to go strangely quiet. She'd heard that when you died things often went into slow motion, and that's obviously what was happening here, since it was so silent she could hear a pin drop (not, of course, that anyone would be dropping a pin right now, but it sure sounded like someone was scraping a chair over in the far corner).

This was not good. And by not good, she meant that she was completely screwed. Normally, Melissa's preferred method of retaliation was through public humiliation, but at Miller Road Elementary, she had occasionally been known to dish out the odd charley horse as well. Sophie shut her eyes and tried to stop her teeth from chattering. *Fear has no place here, fear has no place here,* she chanted to herself.

"Eight," Melissa continued. "Nine, and finally we have... *oh.*"

Sophie, whose eyes were still shut, stiffened. *Oh?* What

did *oh* mean? Did it mean Melissa was going to change her method of punishment?

"Soph," Harvey hissed from somewhere behind her. "I think you should open your eyes."

Really? Because Sophie wasn't so sure; however, she knew she had to face up to it eventually, and so she reluctantly snapped them open just in time to see Melissa holding a Bella's Boutique bag in her hand. A Bella's Boutique bag that had a brand-new pair of jeans, neatly wrapped up in layer upon layer of delicate tissue paper.

Sophie wrinkled her nose.

Okay, so was this some kind of weird joke? She glanced over to Harvey and Kara and shot them a confused look, but the pair of them shook their heads and looked just as astonished as she felt. Not that Melissa noticed any of this because she was far too busy meticulously inspecting the Motion jeans that were now in her hands. However, she finally finished, and after carefully folding them back up and slipping them into the carrier bag, she turned to Sophie.

"Well, I must admit, I didn't think you were going to come through."

That would make two of them, and Sophie blinked. "S-so does that mean we're okay now?"

"Please, we're hardly okay, and don't think for one minute that I'll be forgetting about this. But since you've given me a new pair of jeans, I won't be mentioning this matter to anyone. Though"—she suddenly narrowed her eyes—"if I ever see you anywhere near my house again, I can assure you that you'll be sorry."

Then without another word she turned and started to saunter away to where her minions (Harvey liked to call them the Tait-bots) were waiting for her. Sophie immediately felt her knees start to wobble, and she staggered back to join Kara and Harvey at their table.

"Um, so what just happened there?" Sophie looked at them both helplessly. "I mean, one minute I was preparing for a horrible and completely painful death, and the next minute—"

"The next minute a bag with a pair of jeans suddenly appeared in Melissa's hands." Kara rubbed her eyes for a moment as if to check that they were working properly.

"I mean, it was literally from nowhere," Harvey added, his voice full of awe. "You should've seen Melissa's face. It was like she had just been given a bag of snakes. Whatever it was she had planned for you must've been pretty gruesome, and she almost seemed disappointed that you came through like that."

"Yes, but how did you come through like that?" Kara wrinkled her brow. "I thought that you spent all your money."

"I did." Sophie nodded as she rubbed her brow. "Not to mention the fact that I'd completely forgotten about it all. So where did the jeans come from?"

"I don't know." Harvey picked up the spoon from his Jell-O and started to tap it against his chin. "Melissa said that you either had to give her the money or the jeans, and then—"

"Then Sophie said that she 'wished' she could," Kara finished off, her eyes wide. For a minute Sophie felt like a million little spots were dancing in front of her eyes, but she ignored them as she stared at her friend.

"Okay, so you seriously think that I did that?" she asked. "Because that's crazy."

"Well, it's not that crazy," Harvey reasoned. "I mean, yesterday you found out you were a djinn, and today you granted a wish. Of course, according to the movies, you normally grant wishes to other people, whereas this wish seemed to be for you, but all the same, it sort of makes sense."

"But I didn't do anything. There was no nose twitching or hand waving or anything. All I said was that I wished it would happen, and then it did happen. Plus, remember that Malik said I couldn't access my powers until the djinn ring was cleansed." Sophie unconsciously started to twist the ring that was on her finger. "But then again, he also said that all djinns lied, himself included, so perhaps he just made it all up? *And did I really just do some magic?*"

"Well, it does seem like it." Kara glanced over to where Melissa Tait was sitting, surrounded by her Tait-bots, still holding the bag of jeans. "Hey, why don't you try wishing for something else? That way we'll know if it is just one of those bizarre coincidences or not."

"You think this could be a coincidence?" Harvey

spluttered. "Because in my book, a coincidence is when two people sit down on the bus and discover that they're reading the same book. When a two-hundred-buck pair of jeans turn up out of nowhere, that's a whole different league."

"Okay, so it wasn't a coincidence," Kara conceded as she started to get her stubborn look on her face. "But I still think that Sophie should try it again and see what happens."

"But what should I wish for?"

"I don't know. Anything." Kara shrugged.

"No." Harvey looked at them in alarm. "Not anything. Just something small. Like a... oh, like a Snickers bar."

"Harvey, stop thinking about your stomach," Kara said.

"I'm not," he protested. "It's just, what if it works and Sophie goes and wishes for Neanderthal Joe to turn up in the cafeteria? How on earth would we explain that one away?"

"As if I would." Sophie rolled her eyes. Besides, she had been thinking more along the lines of another pair of jeans in case she bumped into Jonathan Tait again today, but she had to admit that Harvey had a point and that something small would be better. "Okay, I'll wish for a Snickers bar, and then we can—"

However, before she could even finish the sentence a Snickers bar suddenly appeared in the middle of the table. For a moment the three of them were silent as Harvey opened it up and cautiously sniffed it. Then he took a small bite out of the corner and looked up at them both.

"Yup, that's a Snickers bar." He took another bite, obviously to clarify the situation, before he wrinkled his brow. "So what should we do now?"

"I'll tell you what we should do." Sophie felt her whole body start to tingle with energy and excitement as she silently wished for a new iPod. A second later a bright pink Nano (16 GB) appeared in front of her. She picked it up and turned it over in awe as she noted that it had all of Neanderthal Joe's albums already downloaded onto it.

"Well, don't keep us in suspense. What's the plan?" Kara demanded, and Sophie grinned as she held up some Skullcandy headphones so that her friends could have a listen.

"The plan is to have some fun."

12

I DON'T LIKE IT." HARVEY LEANED OVER TO WHERE Sophie was busy conjugating some Spanish verbs in their final class of the day.

"Really?" Sophie put down her pencil and glanced down at the new Chucky Ts he was now wearing. "I thought the green was cute. They sort of match your eyes; plus, weren't they the ones you saw in the mall the other day? Not that it matters, because if you'd like another color, then that's okay."

"No." Harvey shook his straight hair and held up his hand to stop her. "It's not the color. It's the everything." He waved his hand in the air, probably to indicate the new leather-bound sketch pad that Kara was reverently patting. Not to mention Sophie's new boyfriend-cut jeans that she had seen in this month's *Girl2day* magazine (okay, and the coordinating boots, because really it would be a shame to have one and not the other). "I don't like all the magic."

"Why not?" Sophie pushed a strand of hair out of her face before realizing it would be easier just to get a new hair clip. A second later a tortoiseshell barrette was in her hand. She slipped it in. *Ah, that was better.*

"Excuse me, but is there something we should know about?" their new Spanish teacher, Señor Rena, called out from the front of the class. Sophie quickly stopped fiddling with the hair clip and shook her head. She had known that Señor Rena would be a problem ever since she had discovered he was only five feet four and had a bald patch. Short, bald teachers were always cranky. Fact.

"Because," Harvey continued in a low voice once their teacher had returned his attention to the whiteboard. "Remember all those articles I found that said that magic has a real cause and effect. I just think we need to know more about it first. Find out what it means."

"Well, as far as I can tell, it means I can do magic," Sophie explained to him before grinning again. "So seriously, do you want me to change the sneakers or not?"

"No I don't want you to change the sneakers. I want you to listen to me," Harvey persisted in a whisper. He paused for a moment as Señor Rena stopped writing; however, when he didn't turn around, Harvey continued, "I just think you should be careful with this stuff until you know more about it."

"Yes, but that's not my fault," Sophie reminded him in an equally low voice as she held up her hands to prove how red they were from clapping. In fact, they had spent the rest of their lunch break crammed into the janitor's closet (which, for the record, always seemed to be completely empty of janitors). But despite all the clapping that she'd done, there had been no sign of Malik. Not that Sophie had really minded because she was far too eager to see what else she could do with her new power.

And to think that this time yesterday she had thought that being a djinn was the worst thing in the world. Just went to show you what a positive mind-set could achieve.

"Yes, well, you haven't exactly been trying hard now," Harvey persisted.

"That's because we're in class, and trust me, no good could possibly come from Malik turning up now."

"Excuse me." Señor Rena spun around again, but before he could continue, the final bell rang and everyone started to pack their books away. For a moment Sophie thought the teacher was going to call her over, but instead he just shot her the universal "I'll be watching you from now on, Missy" look before he stalked out of the class as fast as his short legs would carry him.

Still, Sophie was too happy to really care, and if he tried to get mad at her tomorrow, perhaps she would just conjure him up some extra hair. That should make him happy.

"Are you two crazy?" Kara hissed from Sophie's other side as the rest of the class started to pile out past them. "I almost thought you were both going to get a detention on the second day of school. What were you talking about... oh, is that a new hair clip? Pretty."

"*That's* what I was talking about," Harvey said in a dry voice as he finished scooping his books into his bag and got to his feet. "I just think that Sophie needs to hold off on all the abracadabra until we know more about it."

"What's there to know?" Sophie demanded in surprise. "I mean, this is seriously the best thing ever. Ever, ever."

"My point exactly." Harvey slung his backpack over his shoulder, and they all made their way out of the school and toward the school bus. "There's got to be a catch. I mean, if it was so easy to do, then why did Malik tell you that it wasn't possible yet? What was the submarine analogy that he used?"

"Okay, so yes, I know he said I wouldn't be able to do magic yet, but he was obviously wrong. And actually, I would bet money that it wouldn't be the first time he was wrong. Not to mention crazy. Did I tell you that he thinks that the reason Cheetos are orange is because mankind wanted to show how much they respect and honor djinns?"

"I still think there's a catch." A stubborn scowl tugged around Harvey's mouth.

"Like what?" Sophie wanted to know as she just avoided being flattened by Ben Griggs as he pushed his way past them and raced over to where Melissa Tait was standing underneath a huge sycamore tree (in her new Motion jeans), surrounded by her Tait-bots. "Because the catch can't be that I only get three wishes, since I used them up way back at the cafeteria when I conjured up that necklace for Kara."

"Which I love." Kara's hand immediately flew to the tiny silver paintbrush that was hanging from a chain around her neck.

"Yes, there could be another catch," Harvey went on as the worry lines continued to march across his brow with military precision. "I watched this horror movie once, and every time this one person did magic, somewhere else in the world, someone suffered because of it."

"Harvey." Sophie rolled her eyes.

"What? It's true," he insisted before conceding. "Well, okay so it was true in that movie."

"Well, I don't think it's true for Sophie," Kara pointed out.

"Fine, but I also saw this other movie where all the magic started to fade away like an illusion," he continued, and this time Sophie did feel a stab of panic go darting through her.

"W-what do you mean?" She fanned her face. "Are you saying that the stuff I've made won't last?"

"I don't know," he admitted with a shake of his nut brown hair. "I'm just saying that it's possible, and that until you speak to Malik that you should really hold off on using it."

Sophie looked over to where Melissa Tait was talking to Ben Griggs while striking various poses in her new jeans. If those jeans disappeared, then it would be fair to say that Melissa Tait would do more than just give Sophie a charley horse.

"Okay. You've convinced me." Sophie started to clap as they all piled onto the school bus. A few people looked at her oddly, but that would be nothing compared to what they would do if her new clothes (not to mention her new underwear) disappeared. *"Where is he?"*

"Perhaps he just didn't hear you?" Kara suggested in her typical kindhearted way.

"Well, if he didn't, then he's the only one," Harvey retorted as he rubbed his ears. "Do you really need to clap so loudly?"

"Hey, if you hadn't freaked me out, then I wouldn't be clapping at all," Sophie reminded him as she clapped some more. "I would be sitting here enjoying my newfound powers, but no, you had to go and watch all of those weird horror movies and get me all concerned."

Harvey flushed. "You're right. I'm sorry. But while we're waiting for Malik, we can always start going through all of the notes I printed out. We might be able to find something else in there."

"Great idea. Count me in." Kara immediately nodded. "I've already told my mom that I was probably going to your house anyway."

"And my folks have been fighting about who has to take the budgie, so I'm in no hurry to go home. Will your mom mind?"

"Of course not. She was doing an early shift, so she should be home by now. But be warned, if she offers you a chocolate brownie, say no because she's been going onto a weird Web site for single parents, and someone there gave her a really bad brownie recipe. I'm talking rocklike."

"Thanks for the heads-up." Harvey wiped his brow as they stepped inside. Then he frowned. "Why are Meg's legs sticking out the end of the couch like that?"

"No idea." Sophie shook her head as she looked over to where Meg was once again half hidden from sight. "But if it will stop her bugging us, then I'm okay with it. Anyway, if you guys want to head upstairs to my room, I'll just let my mom know we're home."

There was no sign of her mom anywhere, so Sophie hurried out to the small shed at the back of the overgrown garden that her mom used as a pottery studio—well, had used as a pottery studio. These days she didn't tend to go in there much, and when she did, it was more to mope around than to do any work. Sophie was just about to step inside before she remembered that this morning when she left for school, she hadn't been wearing new jeans or boots (or have a double-stitched pink-and-white polka-dot Quiksilver backpack hanging off her shoulder), and so she paused for a moment and wished that she had her old clothes on.

A second later Mr. Jaws, who had been busy sunning himself by the shed door, jumped onto all four paws and hissed at her. Sophie closed her eyes for a moment, and the next thing a bowl of Pretty Kitty Snacks appeared on the ground. Mr. Jaws shot her one final glare before he turned his attention to the food. It was good to see that even cranky, bad-tempered black and white cats had their price.

Sophie took a second to check that her old clothes were all in order and then stepped inside. The shed had once been a place where the whole family had gravitated, but now the secondhand chairs that Mr. Jaws had almost clawed to death were sitting in the corner, unused, while the large pottery wheel in the center of the room was covered with a dusty throw cloth.

Sophie's mom was over in the far corner, standing in front of the floor-to-ceiling shelves where she used to put all of her pottery when it came out of the kiln. The shelves were half empty now, and her mom was holding an old wonky vase in her hand, lovingly tracing the awkward shape with one fingertip.

For a moment Sophie felt her mouth go dry as she recognized the blue-glazed creation.

It was one that her dad had made, and at the time her mom had jokingly told him that he should stick to the cooking and she would stick to pottery. Despite being able to see her mom only from behind, Sophie had a terrible feeling that she had been crying, and she was just about to slip back out when her mom suddenly turned around.

"Oh, honey, I didn't realize you were home already."

Her mom discreetly dabbed at her eyes. "How was school?"

Great. The boy of my dreams sorta, kinda asked me out, and then I discovered that all I need to do is wish for something and then it happens. Of course, the downside is that I'm not quite sure how well the magic will hold up, which is why I need to talk to my djinn guide ASAP.

"Oh, it was okay," she said instead, with what she hoped was a casual shrug.

"Did you find out about where the Neanderthal Joe tickets are going to be sold?" her mom asked. Sophie hadn't planned to tell her mom about them last night, not just because she was distracted by the whole orange/djinn thing but because she no longer could afford to go to the concert. Unfortunately, someone who had gone into the antiques store yesterday had mentioned it, and so Sophie had been forced to confirm it. "Because I'm starting work at ten tomorrow, so I could always go early and pick some up for you. I know how long you've been saving up for it."

"Actually, Kara's mom is going to get them for us. She works right next door," Sophie quickly interposed as she suddenly realized that perhaps it hadn't been such a great idea to talk nonstop all summer about how she was saving up, on the off chance that the Joes put out some extra tickets for the concert. Still, all she had to say was that they couldn't get tickets and then act all upset about it for a couple of days (which wouldn't be too much of a stretch, since the fact she couldn't go would probably end up killing her). *Oh, and it was probably a good idea to change the subject as well.* "Anyway, Harvey and Kara are going to hang out here for a while. Is that okay? Harvey's folks are still fighting."

"Poor Harvey. Such a nice boy. Perhaps some of my brownies will cheer him up?"

"Actually, we had a massive lunch today, so we're not really that hungry."

"Since when is Harvey not hungry?" Her mom lifted a surprised eyebrow.

Since I warned him that they were like rocks, Sophie silently added before giving a vague wave of her hand. "I guess there's a first time for everything. Anyway, I'd better go up."

"Okay then." Her mom nodded before suddenly narrowing her eyes. "Are you all right? You look a bit...different?"

"Really?" Sophie squeaked as she quickly checked her arms to make sure they were the right color. Check. She glanced down to check that her clothes hadn't disappeared. Check. Then she suddenly wondered if something else bad had happened. Did using magic leave some sort of mark on her? Or worse, turn her orange again? Where was Malik when she needed him? "I'm fine. Completely and utterly fine. Never been better."

"Well, just ignore me then, I'm probably just being overprotective." Her mom gave her a sad smile and turned her attention back to the wonky vase and her own private world of pain.

That was way too close. Sophie wiped her brow, ignored Mr. Jaws, who was still hissing at her as she raced back across the yard, and finally reached the safety of her bedroom, where Harvey was already on the Internet and Kara had the printouts spread out across the bed.

"Have you found anything?" she asked in a hopeful voice, but the pair of them shook their heads.

"Not yet. But are you okay? You've gone all pale," he said in concern, dragging his attention away from the screen.

"My mom was just looking at me strangely, like she could tell something was wrong, which then made me worry that perhaps the magic put some weird mark on my face. Do you see anything?"

"No." Kara shook her head. "You are completely weird mark free. In fact—"

The rest of her words were cut off as Malik's newly acquired Zac Efron face suddenly appeared through the middle of her bedroom wall, much like a mounted moose head in a hunting lodge. For a moment he paused and gave them a toothy grin before he stepped all the way through the wall and spread out his arms as if expecting applause.

"Finally. Where have you been?" Sophie instantly demanded, her panic giving away to annoyance. Then she blinked as she realized that while Malik was still wearing his purple harem pants, his top half was now covered in what looked like Meg's favorite My Little Pony T-shirt. *The My Little Pony T-shirt that was designed to fit a six-year-old kid.* "Why are you wearing my sister's clothing?"

"This is your sister's?" Malik blinked. "Huh. Well, I didn't know that. I just found it in the laundry basket this morning and thought it looked cute. It does, right?"

"No, it most definitely does not," Sophie assured him. "And why didn't you come when I first clapped at school?"

"Ah, well, you see, I bumped into Eric the Giant. He died a hundred years ago when a Zebula curse went wrong. Anyway, he's a great guy. Real funny—oh, but never play cards with him. Not if you want to keep your camel. Actually, that's another rule. Never gamble with other djinns. Cheaters every single one of them. You should write that down."

Sophie glared at him, while next to her Harvey jumped to his feet, his face deathly white. Next to him Kara's eyes were bulging.

"Okay, so whoa!" Harvey pointed. "I mean, it's not that I didn't believe you about all of this, but whoa. A real-life djinn? Well... actually a real-life *dead* djinn."

"A dead djinn who looks like Zac Efron," Kara added in awe. Sophie had explained to her friends about Malik's transformation, but it was obvious by Kara's face that she hadn't expected it to be quite so Zac-like.

"How come they can both see you?" Sophie double-checked, since it suddenly occurred to her that if her friends could see him, then perhaps her mom could as well, and no good could come from that.

"It's because I'm allowing them to," Malik said as he snapped his fingers and suddenly disappeared from sight. "See what I did there," he yelled out in a disembodied voice before reappearing a second later with a large grin on his face. "Nifty, huh? Oh, and what about this?"

This time when he snapped his fingers, Zac Efron was gone and in his place was Selena Gomez, still wearing the same outfit. Kara didn't look quite so happy, but Harvey's jaw fell to the floor as his eyes widened. Sophie was pretty sure there was even some drool.

"It's not real." She nudged him, which seemed to shake Harvey from his stunned trance.

"Well, at least it's nice to see that some people appreciate my talents." Malik nodded to Harvey as he smoothed down the My Little Pony T-shirt. Then he narrowed his eyes. "Anyway, did you want me for something? Don't tell me you grew a tail?"

"What?" Sophie stared at him in alarm. "What do you... *oh, never mind.* I called you here because suddenly I seem to be able to do magic, despite the fact that you told me I definitely wouldn't be able to do anything until my djinn ring was cleansed."

"That is correct." He nodded, and Sophie made a growling noise.

"No." She shook her head. "It's not correct. That's what I'm saying. All I need to do is say the words *'I wish'* and—"

"Oooooh." Malik made a tut-tutting noise and shook his head. "You should never say the words *'I wish.'* Well, obviously I can say them, because I'm dead as a dodo (though not nearly as stupid). But for you, that's a big no-no. Actually, you should write that down. Rule number one about being a new djinn. Never say the words 'I wish' until you know how to control your powers properly."

"And you didn't think to mention this yesterday?" Sophie raised an eyebrow and used her hands to fan her face. "Since I've just spent a whole afternoon wishing stuff up."

"You've been conjuring stuff up?" Malik looked surprised. "Are you sure about that?"

"Yes, I'm sure. Why would I tell you if I didn't really do it?"

"How should I know?" He shrugged. "Though I've noticed that you have the habit of getting quite dramatic. Perhaps you merely think you've been doing it?"

"Oh, I've been doing it all right." Then, before Malik could open his mouth again, she closed her eyes and concentrated on his ill-fitting T-shirt. When she opened them again, it was bye-bye My Little Pony and hello plain navy Gap shirt.

"Okay, so I didn't see that one coming." Malik let out a long whistling noise as studied the polo shirt for a moment before shooting Sophie an impressed glance. "To be honest, I didn't think you'd be able to manage anything like this so quickly, which is why I didn't go into detail about it. Plus, I really was hungry yesterday, but I can see that you're far more talented than I expected. So tell me, how did you do it?"

"I just wished that you had on a different shirt, and bingo." Sophie shrugged before widening her eyes. "Actually, while we're at it, you should really lose those harem pants. I wi—"

"Whoa." Malik suddenly held up his hands to silence her. "Hey, hey, hey. What part of my little 'You shouldn't say the words *I wish* speech' didn't you understand?"

"I thought that was only because I didn't know how to control my powers. But since it seems that I do, I figured it was okay."

"Well, it's definitely *not* okay." He waggled his finger at her. "In fact, unless it's an absolute life-or-death emergency, you really shouldn't do anything with your powers until your ring is cleansed and you've mastered your exercises."

"What exercises?"

"Oh, did I not give them to you?" Malik looked surprised as he fumbled around in the pocket of his harem pants and pulled out a crumpled paper napkin that had some messy writing on it. "Huh. Well, what do you know? Anyway, you need to start practicing this right away. They will help give you the control you need."

Sophie took the napkin and smoothed it out. She studied it for a moment before looking up at Malik. "I need to practice one latte and a pastrami on rye?"

"Oh, no, that was my lunch order." Malik waved his hand. "But the rest of the stuff is all legitimate."

"Meditate while standing on my head?" Sophie read out. "Visualize a golden orb of Phatatuela? Chant a strange sentence with too many *r*'s in it a hundred times a day?"

"Not as easy as it sounds," Malik assured her. "Especially if you have a lisp. Anyway, if you do too much conjuring without having the right control, then there can be side effects. Now, if that's everything, I should probably get going. Eric the Giant knows this great restaurant that we were going to check out."

"Side effects?" Harvey's eyes bulged in panic, no doubt thanks to his watching way too many horror movies. "Like what?"

"Her head will probably explode." Malik shrugged before grinning at their horrified expressions. "I kid. I kid. Honestly, you guys need to try to relax a bit more. Talk about Generation Overreact Much. I'm referring to headaches, itchy elbows, that sort of thing."

"That's it?" Even Harvey looked disappointed.

"You've obviously not had an itchy elbow before," Malik retorted with a sniff. "It's no laughing matter. Do you understand?"

"Yes. Fine." Sophie reluctantly nodded. "I need to steer clear of conjuring anything until my djinn ring is fully cleansed and I've practiced all of my exercises."

"Correct. Exercise, exercise, exercise. That's the key." Malik nodded as he glanced at a large plastic watch that was strapped to his wrist. It looked remarkably like something straight out of *Ben 10*. "And seriously, I really got to dash. That all-you-can-eat buffet isn't going to stay full of shrimp all night. But remember. No more conjuring, unless it's for an absolute emergency. Are we clear?"

"Of course." Sophie gave her an adamant nod of her head. "One hundred percent, crystal clear."

13

"I DON'T THINK I'VE SEEN THAT T-SHIRT BEFORE." Sophie's mom frowned the following morning as she looked up from the scrambled eggs she was stirring. "Is it new?"

"Of course not." Sophie instantly sat down at the table and crossed her fingers. Not that it was exactly a lie since, while it might've been brand new last night, today, well, it wasn't quite so new. And Mr. Jaws could stop with all the hissing, too, because she didn't care what anyone said, getting a new shirt for the third day of school was an absolute emergency.

Besides, after Harvey had gone home yesterday, her mom's boss Mr. Rivers had come around with a huge stack of papers, and he and her mom had been holed up in the kitchen all night. Sophie had managed to slip off to her room to work on the exercises that Malik had given her—not to mention use the lotion Rufus had sent to carefully cleanse her djinn ring with—take her anti-orange potion, and surf the Internet to see what else she could find out about her new powers. And then there was her homework (which, considering it was only the first week back at school, seemed more than a little extreme).

So really, she was feeling quite virtuous right now. Especially since she had been longing to get a cool cardigan to go with the shirt, but she had rather heroically decided not to. And as for—

"Earth to Sophie," her mom cut into her thoughts as she walked over to the table holding the frying pan in front of her. "Did you even hear what I just said?"

"Huh?" Sophie blinked as she realized she had been daydreaming. "Sorry, I was, er…thinking about my Spanish homework. What were you saying?"

"I was saying that I'll give you a lift to school today because I'm worried about Meg, so I thought I'd talk to her new teacher. How has Meg seemed to you? Has she been behaving herself after school?"

"Yes, she's been good," Sophie quickly said since her mom was looking worried. And besides, who was to say that there was anything wrong with lying under a couch and watching shark documentaries?

"No, I haven't been good." Meg suddenly piped up from over by the doorway. "I've been bad. You should make me stay home from school as punishment."

"Honey, we've been through this." Her mom finished dishing out the breakfast. "And I promise that soon it will get easier, until one day you will actually find that you want to go to school."

Meg might've been only six, but she wasn't buying it for a minute. "Yeah, right," Sophie's little sister muttered as she sulkily sat down at the table and looked at the food on her plate. "Why can't I have Coco Pops?"

"Because you can't," her mom said in a patient voice as she picked up her coffee cup and rejoined them at the table. "And just because you ask for the same things every morning, it doesn't mean you will get them. Now while you girls are eating your breakfast, there's something I need to talk to you both about."

Sophie, who had been giving the scrambled eggs an unenthusiastic prod, looked up in surprise. She had completely forgotten that her mom had wanted to "talk" to them. Mind you, the thought of losing her broadband wasn't quite as daunting as it had been yesterday, since now that she had magic, she would be able to zap them up some more.

"What about?" Sophie asked as Meg poked out her bottom lip and looked like she was going to cry. Sophie reached out to squeeze her little sister's hand, but before she could do so, there was a spluttering noise from over by the kitchen bench and she looked up to see Malik/Zac standing there pulling faces at the remaining eggs, which were still sitting in the pan.

"Oh my freak show. What are you doing here?" she yelped before she could catch herself. The minute she did so, she put her hand over her mouth to stop any more words from coming out. But seriously, this was bad.

Not that Malik even seemed to notice the chaos he was causing as he glanced over at her.

"I'm looking at this stuff," he explained to her before wrinkling his nose. "What on earth is it? Because I've been around for a long, long time, and I've never seen anything that looks this bad. And that includes the time my buddy Philippe the Red Terror made us all eat buttered-rat casserole. What? Why are you looking at me like that? It's true," Malik insisted before finally figuring something out. "Oh, right, you're worried about their seeing me—well, don't be. I'm completely invisible to them. Though apparently that cat can sense that something's up. What's his problem anyway?"

Sophie looked over to where Mr. Jaws was going into hiss overdrive, and she felt like she was going to be sick.

"Honey, who are you talking to?" Her mom looked over to where Malik was standing and Sophie started to fan her face down with her hand; thankfully, he must've been telling the truth (for once), since her mom seemed oblivious to the fact there was a ghost in the kitchen, and instead she swiveled back around and gave Sophie a concerned glance. "Is everything okay?"

"What?" Sophie blinked as she got to her feet while making a mental note to kill Malik. "I mean, yes, everything's fine. I was just practicing something for school. A-and speaking of school, I've just remembered there's something I need to get. From my room," she added as she shot Malik a pointed glare.

"But you haven't finished your breakfast, not to mention the fact there's something important I need to talk to you about."

Fortunately, before Sophie could even start to explain why she didn't care about getting rid of the broadband as long as she could get Malik out of the kitchen, the phone rang. She only just stopped herself from giving the Universe a big thumbs-up in gratitude.

"Fine." Her mom let out a sigh as she stood up to look for the cordless phone. "But we're leaving in ten minutes, okay?"

"Okay," Sophie instantly agreed before she raced over to where Malik was still making faces at the eggs. She shot him a mutinous look.

"Boy, you really aren't a morning person, are you?" he complained, but he seemed happy to follow her out of the room and back upstairs. Well, she intended for him to follow, but really he just disappeared from sight and was waiting for her, cross-legged on the corner of her bed, when she pushed open her door.

"Are you insane?" she demanded in a low voice in case Meg had decided to tag along behind her. "What are you doing coming into the kitchen like that? You scared me."

"Was it the Zac thing? Perhaps I should've just come in as myself? Or a panda bear. They're so cute, no one can be scared by a panda." As he spoke he clicked his fingers and for one terrifying minute, Sophie thought that a panda was going to appear in her room. But thankfully he just seemed to be smoothing down his perfect Zac Efron hair.

"It's not the shape-shifting. It's the turning up when my family is around. You can't do that."

"I was hungry," Malik protested. "And I mistakenly thought I could get some food from down there. Boy was I wrong. How do you eat that stuff?"

"Normally, we make our own breakfast, but because it's the first week back at school, Mom feels like she should cook for us."

"Well, she shouldn't." Malik gave a decisive shake of his head. "Not ever."

"Hey, you're preaching to the choir on that one," Sophie assured him before narrowing her eyes. "And besides, that's not really the point. The point is that you can't just come and wander around the house anytime you like. Anyway, don't let me keep you from whatever it is you do all day when I'm not around."

"Actually"—Malik glanced over to the computer—"I was thinking of staying here and having a go on that thing while you're at school?"

"You want to surf the Internet?" Sophie asked in surprise.

"No, I want to look at that magic screen of yours," Malik corrected, and Sophie only just stopped herself from rolling her eyes.

"And if I let you, you won't go wandering around the

house or anything like that?" she double-checked.

"Djinn's honor." He held up his fingers in some sort of complicated salute that Sophie was pretty sure he had just made up. However, he looked earnest enough, and also, if he was here at the house, at least she would know how to get to him if she had any more djinn emergencies (not that she would, of course, because they were a thing of the past). She let out a reluctant sigh.

"Okay, fine," Sophie said as she took the mouse out of his hand and put it back onto the table so she could show him how to use it. A few minutes later Malik nodded as she explained how Google worked. "Understand?"

"Sure." Malik gave a vague wave of his hand before suddenly turning around and shooting her a winning smile. "Though, actually, one more thing. Could you conjure me up some of those Cheetos?"

"What?" Sophie looked at him.

"It's just that I'm hungry, but I've already promised not to go wandering around the house." As he spoke he did some sort of pout thing that might have worked if he was six, but right now it just looked like a two-thousand-year-old dead ghost stuck in Zac Efron's body. In other words, it wasn't a good look.

"Is this some sort of test?" She narrowed her eyes at him.

"Test? Why would you say that? I don't understand?" Malik looked confused.

"Well, yesterday you told me not to use my powers, blah, blah, blah, and now you want me to zap you up some junk food."

"I would hardly call those divine sticks of cheesy goodness junk," Malik protested. "And besides, this is an exception."

"Why? Because it's for you?" Sophie rolled her eyes.

"Exactly. Rule number one. Always do what your djinn guide asks you to do." Malik nodded in delight as he held his hand out for the Cheetos, but when Sophie still didn't do anything, he narrowed his eyes. "Besides, don't think I can't recognize a newly conjured T-shirt when I see one. Or for that matter the new stationery that's currently sitting in your bag. Of course, I could reprimand you for your using your powers when I instructed you not to . . . or I could choose to overlook it just this once."

"Fine." Sophie let out a sigh and closed her eyes for a moment. When she opened them, there were twenty packets of Cheetos sitting on her bed and Malik was rubbing his hands in excitement.

"Well done," Malik congratulated her as he collected them all and stuffed them under his bulging T-shirt so the he looked more like Homer Simpson than a ghost "Don't forget to clap if you need me."

"Yeah, because that works so well," Sophie retorted, but before she could say anything else, her mom called out to say that it was time to go.

★ ★ ★ ★ ★

"So I've got this for you," Harvey said as they walked down the corridor at lunchtime. As he spoke, he handed her a piece of paper that had some kind of chart on it, with lots of different colors all over it.

"What is it?" Sophie looked at him blankly.

"It's a flowchart, to help you remember to do all of your ring cleansing and meditation," Harvey explained as he began to point out the lines and colors. "It seems like there is a lot to remember—not to mention all the homework and stuff—so I thought this might help. Plus, my folks were arguing last night, and the printer helped block out some of the noise."

"Harvey, this is so nice of you," Sophie said as she took the chart and then giggled as she noticed that he'd even included a break so that she could listen to some Neanderthal Joe music.

"I just didn't want you to think that I wasn't being helpful. I mean, I knew what was happening, but it wasn't until I really saw Malik with my own two eyes—"

"You mean Selena," Sophie teased, and Harvey's face immediately brightened.

"Okay, so that part was just weird. But anyway, I figured this might help you get through it all."

"Well, I really appreciate it," she said as they reached her locker. Then she frowned as she realized that Harvey was looking at her strangely. "Are you okay? Why are you doing that thing with your eyebrows?"

"Er, because I suddenly remembered that I was supposed to be meeting Kara, and you know what she's like if you're late," he said, and then took off without another word. Which was weird since Kara never cared two hoots if anyone was late or not. Sophie was just about to go racing after her friend to check if everything was all right when there was a coughing noise from behind her and she spun around to see Jonathan Tait standing next to her locker.

"Oh, hey. I didn't see you there," she stammered as she watched him use his left hand to brush his perfect hair out of his perfect eyes. For a moment she grinned as she remembered that yesterday, on this very spot, he had sortofkindofmaybe asked her out to the Neanderthal Joe concert.

However, her grin started to fade as she then remembered something else. And that was, despite how nice and gorgeous he was, Jonathan was still Melissa Tait's twin brother, and so there was no way he didn't know about the jeans mix-up. Which, in turn, meant that whatever weird and crazy thing had prompted him yesterday to ask if she wanted to hang out with him at the concert was probably long gone. In fact, he and Melissa had likely started to call her the-crazy-jeans-stealing-babysitter girl, and—

"Are you okay? You're so quiet." He coughed again, and Sophie realized she must've just been standing there staring at him.

"Oh, right, yes, I'm fine," she hastily assured him while

forcing herself not to wish for the ground to swallow her up whole.

"Good." He shot her an adorable grin, which Sophie would've enjoyed a lot more if she didn't know what was coming. "The thing is, I wanted to talk to you about the concert."

"It's okay," she quickly assured him, deciding that the rip-the-Band-Aid-off-quick method was probably the least painful way to do this. "I mean, I totally understand how you must feel, what with the jeans thing and your sister. Not that it was my fault," she hastily added. "You see, Ryan, who I was babysitting, stole my jeans, and I promise you I had absolutely no idea in the world that he had gone into your yard and swapped them over, and—"

"I know," he cut her off. "That kid's a nightmare. In fact, I like to call him the ultimate ev—"

"Evil." Sophie finished off in amazement. "Yeah, me, too."

"And I told Melissa that it was probably Ryan who took her jeans, but unfortunately, logical thinking and good listening aren't really two of my sister's strong points."

Sophie blinked. "Are you serious?"

"What? That my sister isn't always the nicest person in the Universe? I've sort of had twelve years of proof. I mean, she has her moments when she's okay, but they are so few and far between, most of the time I just tend to stay out of her way. So anyway, back to the concert. Did you manage to get tickets?"

Sophie was about to shake her head and tell him no, but before she could, he pulled a wide blue ticket out of his pocket and showed it to her. Sophie's eyes widened at how gorgeous it was. There was even a hologram on it, and she looked longingly at it for a moment before Jonathan started to study his sneakers (and nice sneakers they were as well, just like the ones she had zapped up for Harvey but blue instead of green).

"I spoke to my brother, and he's cool with taking you and your friends along. And my mom said that she would call yours to make sure it was okay."

"Really? But what about Melissa?"

"She would rather rip off her arm and eat it than be seen at an NJ concert," he assured her, and for a moment Sophie just stared at the ticket. Then she looked up at Jonathan and stared at him some more. He was so gorgeous and so nice, and did she mention gorgeous? Plus, what were the chances of this situation ever happening again? Never, that's what. This was her one and only chance to see the Joes in the company of Jonathan Tait, and if that didn't constitute an emergency, then she didn't know what did. "So do you want to come with us?"

"Of course we do," Sophie said in a rush before she could change her mind. Then, after pausing for a moment to shut her eyes and make a wish, she pulled three pristine, identical Neanderthal Joe tickets out of her back pocket. "There's nothing my friends and I would like more. In fact, it would be awesome."

14

MEG, HOW MANY TIMES HAVE I TOLD YOU NOT TO come into my room?" Sophie complained the following morning when she heard the door open and looked over to discover her little sister standing in front of her. Of course, considering Sophie was on her head trying to do one of the exercises Malik had given her, Meg appeared to be upside down, but that was beside the point. The point was that she shouldn't be in the room at all. Sophie let her legs fall down and collapsed in a heap on the floor next to Harvey's flowchart.

"Mom wants to know why it's taking you so long to come down to breakfast," Meg said, as if that made it okay. Then she wandered over to the nightstand next to Sophie's bed. In between the photos and the small silver box that Sophie's dad had given her long ago, there was an article that Malik had printed out yesterday from Rufus the Furious's Web site when he had been on his computer marathon. Naturally, Meg picked it up. "What's this? And why is there a picture of an orange person on it?"

"It's nothing." Sophie scrambled into a standing position and snatched the piece of paper out of Meg's hand while letting out a small prayer of thanks that Meg couldn't read properly, since the accompanying text was all about what to expect in your first fifty years as a djinn. (Unfortunately, none of it was remotely helpful unless she cared about being able to attend Djinn Council open days and vote in Djinn Council elections, and she had the feeling that Malik had printed it out only because it had a picture of some female djinn on it who he'd apparently once had a thing for. Gross.)

"Why were you standing on your head?" Meg continued.

"I was meditating. It's what enlightened people do," Sophie retorted as she patted her hair and hoped that the static bird nest that it had become would disappear before she got to school. Actually, she *wished* it would disappear. A second later her blonde hair felt smooth and shiny— and like it had some extra volume to it. Because, well, just because...

Then she realized that Meg was still looking at her. "Can you please stop asking so many questions."

"Why?" Meg instantly asked, but Sophie ignored her as she hurried downstairs to where their mom was once again burning something in a saucepan. She couldn't wait for next week when they could all return to toast and cereal.

"I thought you were never going to come down," her mom said as Sophie grabbed a glass of orange juice.

"Sorry." She drank the juice in three long gulps. "I didn't realize the time."

"Because she was standing on her head so the clock was upside down," Meg added in a helpful voice. Sophie shot her a dark look.

"Standing on your head?" Her mom raised an eyebrow as she came over to the table with a pan in her hand. "What brought that about?"

"Oh, I just read about it in one of my positive-thinking books. It's a good way to relax," Sophie improvised as she crossed her fingers. The truth was that while Kara and Harvey had been excited to see the Neanderthal Joe tickets yesterday—especially the part on them that said Access All Areas—Kara had also been a bit worried about the fact that Sophie had used yet more magic. Which was weird since it was normally Harvey who worried, but he still didn't quite seem to have recovered since Malik turned himself into Selena Gomez.

Of course, she had tried to explain that the situation was a complete emergency, and even though Kara had eventually admitted that it was pretty cool, it was only after Sophie had promised faithfully to do double the amount of exercises that Malik had given her. Hence the extra head standing.

"Interesting. Perhaps I should give it a go as well?" her mom wondered as she started to push something gray and sludgy onto Meg's plate. Her little sister looked at it in disgust, and even Mr. Jaws started to shudder delicately from his spot over by the window.

"I don't want this." Meg pushed the plate away as a petulant frown made its way onto her face. "It looks disgusting."

"It's oatmeal. It's good for you, so I want you to eat it," her mom insisted as she used the back of her hand to wipe her brow. "Now," she added, as she waited for Meg to unenthusiastically hold a spoonful up to her mouth.

"I still don't want it. I wish I could have Coco Pops," Meg persisted in an unrelenting voice as Sophie felt a wave of pain go racing through her stomach. She immediately doubled over. Ouch, ouch, and ouch.

"Sophie. Are you okay?" Her mom's Worried Mom face went into overdrive, and Sophie waited a moment until the pain and the nausea subsided. She had no idea what had just happened, but she was 100 percent sure that she didn't want it to happen again.

"Yes, I'm fine," she managed to croak as she tried to figure out if it was some kind of djinn thing that Malik had forgotten to mention. "I just got an upset stomach, but it's gone now."

"Are you sure?" Her mom looked even more worried. "I wonder if you should stay home from school today?"

"What?" Meg poked out her lower lip in a mulish frown. "How come she gets to stay home?"

"Because she's sick," her mom said.

"No, I'm not. I'm fine," Sophie insisted, since there was no way she was staying away from school today. Especially since, as promised, Jonathan Tait's mom had called last night to check about the concert, and Sophie's mom had given her the big yes. "Anyway, if I stayed at home, then you'd have to miss work, and you don't want to do that."

"Well, it would be awkward," her mom conceded. "But only if you're sure that you really are okay," she double-checked, then frowned at Meg. "And you, young lady, I'm still waiting for you to eat your oatmeal."

"Fine," Meg muttered as she took a bite. "But that doesn't mean... hey, it does taste like Coco Pops."

"What?" Sophie and her mom both looked at her in surprise. Meg was notoriously grumpy in the morning, and normally it took a lot more than lumpy oatmeal to snap her out of one of her moods, but Meg was too busy shoveling spoonfuls of gray sludge into her mouth to bother answering.

"Let me try that," her mom said as she stuck her pinky into the saucepan and tasted it. Then her eyes widened. "She's right. I've got no idea how that happened. I guess I must've used cocoa instead of cinnamon."

"Well, you should do it again," Meg finally spoke. "Because it's nice."

"Yes, but it's hardly good for you." Her mom put down the saucepan and looked even more stressed than normal. "Which is why—"

But before she could finish, Kara poked her head

around the door, and Sophie jumped to her feet and grabbed her bag.

"Got to fly, but I'll see you this afternoon." Sophie grinned as she hurried out the door to where her friends were waiting. She didn't even need to ask if Mrs. Tait had spoken to their parents because their smiles said it all. Sometimes it was just great to be alive. And to think that she'd been worried about becoming a djinn.

"So tell me again what he said?" Kara whispered in excitement as Señor Rena walked into the room that afternoon just minutes after Sophie had bumped into Jonathan Tait in the corridor. Did she mention that she loved this school?

"He said that he's heard what the concert set list is going to be and that he's going to burn me a CD of it all in the right order." Sophie sighed a happy sigh.

"And have you decided what you're going to wear?" Kara wanted to know, and Sophie grinned.

"Well, it's a toss-up between my new jeans—not my Melissa Tait–tainted new jeans, but the other ones that I conjured up—and my old NJ tour T-shirt that I was wearing when Jonathan first talked to me, *or* my green skirt and... Harvey, seriously, what are you doing?"

They both turned to where Harvey was systematically pulling all the books out of his bag. He looked up at them both and blinked. "Oh, right. I was just feeling hungry, so I was sort of wishing that I still had a candy bar in my...

oh sweet. It's a Twix." He suddenly pulled a candy bar out and gave it a happy kiss just as Sophie doubled over in pain and a wave of nausea hit her. It was almost identical to the one that had hit her in the kitchen.

"Are you okay?" Kara looked at her in concern. "What's wrong?"

"Nothing," Sophie gasped as the pain subsided. "I mean, my stomach hurt for a second, but it's better now."

"Really?" Señor Rena was suddenly by her side. "Are you sure that you wouldn't like to make some more noise and continue to interrupt my class for a bit longer?" he asked, but Sophie, who knew better than to engage in conversation with short, bald, passive-aggressive teachers, quickly shook her head.

"No, Señor Rena."

"Well, good. And since you're so eager to draw attention to yourself, perhaps you would like to stand up and talk about last night's homework questions?"

Sophie gulped as she got to her feet. This was going to be a long lesson.

"Man, Señor Rena was so harsh just then," Kara complained as they piled onto the bus that afternoon.

"I know, right." Sophie nodded. "Mucho harshisimo. But it was funny to see his face when I got all of the homework questions right. Anyway, enough about boring Spanish, let's get back to the concert. We still didn't decide on jeans or skirt."

Harvey rolled his eyes and muttered something about "please just kill me now" before he turned his attention to his unfinished Twix, leaving Sophie and Kara free to spend the rest of the journey home debating how many bracelets was too many bracelets. By the time Sophie waved good-bye to her friends, they had decided that six was definitely enough. She jogged up the front path, humming "Zombie Vegas" to herself.

The black cloud that was coming from the kitchen let her know that her mom was in there cooking, while Meg's legs were once again poking out from under the couch. For a moment she debated whether to go into the kitchen, but as she caught a whiff of the smell that accompanied the black cloud, she decided to go see Meg instead. Because she was in such a good mood, she went and sat down on the floor and tickled her sister's bare feet.

"Get off." Meg immediately flicked her leg.

"What's wrong with you? Don't tell me you still hate first grade?" Sophie wrinkled her nose. "Because you know, Mom's right. It will get better. I mean, look at me. I had the worst start to sixth grade ever. I mean, I'm talking 'Just kill me now and bury the body' sort of stuff, but here we are, a few days later, and not only am I going to see the Joes in concert next Saturday afternoon, but I'm going to hang out with Jonathan Tait as well."

Meg didn't bother to answer and so Sophie, feeling generous, got down on her belly and joined her sister under the couch.

"What I'm trying to say, Meggy-pops, is that you just need to keep a positive attitude and trust that everything will turn out right...hey, what are all these letters doing under here?" As she spoke, she looked at the enormous number of white envelopes that were sitting in neat stacks. She turned her head (not easy when you're stuck under the couch) and stared at Meg. "What's going on? Why are you hiding all of the mail?"

"Because." Meg poked out her bottom lip and added more letters to the pile.

"Because what?" Sophie insisted as she grabbed some of them and wriggled out from under the couch so that she could read them. All the envelopes were addressed to their mom, but in the top left-hand corner of each envelope was a different logo. One was from JK Everest and Son Realtors. Another was from Gibson Property Experts, and a third was from Trenton Real Estate. Sophie immediately grabbed Meg by the ankles and pulled her out from under the couch. "Okay, spill. Tell me what's going on."

"Mom wants to sell the house, and I don't want her to." Meg shot her a defiant look as she reluctantly squirmed up into a sitting position. "So I've been hiding the mail to stop her."

What?

What!

That couldn't be possible.

Their mom couldn't sell the house. Sophie's mouth went dry as all the happy Neanderthal Joe/Jonathan

Tait–induced feelings were replaced by panic. She glanced around the room as her heart thumped like a drum against her ribs. Sophie loved this room. She loved this house.

It's where she and Meg had been born (literally, since their mom and dad hadn't believed in hospitals and had wanted home births, which if you asked Sophie was a little bit gross, and she was very pleased that she had no memories of it). But apart from that one small isolated ick-factor event, she loved everything about their home. Plus, they had to stay in this house for when their dad came back.

How could he come back to them if they moved?

The answer was that he couldn't.

Sophie's throat tightened, and it took all of her willpower even to make the words come out as she finally turned to face Meg. "H-how come you know about this, and I don't?"

"I heard Mom talking to a man about it during the break. You were at Kara's, practicing a dance routine for the new Neanderthal Joe song."

Sophie wrinkled her nose. She remembered going around to practice (before deciding that neither of them could dance to save themselves), but she definitely didn't recall her mom mentioning anything about a real estate agent visiting while she was away.

"Are you sure? I mean, remember that time you thought we were getting free ice cream, but it turned out that Mom was talking about ice cubes instead."

"I'm sure." Meg's small face started to quiver. "The man walked all around, and he said that he would send her an eva…evaul…that he would send her something in the mail."

"So you figured that you would just hide all the mail to stop it from happening," Sophie finished off before she widened her eyes. "Oh my God. Is that why you didn't want to go to school? Because you were afraid she would get the mail before you could?"

Meg nodded as her voice went wobbly. "I asked Trevor to not deliver until after school, but he said it was against the rules. Plus, it would make him late to watch his favorite soap opera."

"Why didn't you tell me?" Sophie shook her head as she put her arms around her little sister while she tried to fight down her nausea.

"'Cause every time Mom tried to talk to you about it, you didn't look that bothered. I didn't think you cared."

"I thought she wanted to get rid of broadband." Sophie let go of her sister and buried her head in her hands for a moment. "I had no idea she would ever try to sell the house. She can't sell the house. This is awful."

"So does that mean you'll help me with the mail?" Meg asked in a hopeful voice. "Because I think I need a better hiding place."

"Meg, we can't keep hiding the mail forever. Eventually, these people will just come around or call."

"Who will come around?" her mom's voice suddenly said, and Sophie looked up to see her walking into the room. "Hello, honey, I didn't realize you were home yet. Is everything okay? You look like you've seen a ghost."

Actually, seeing a ghost was easy and almost completely painless (apart from when Malik went on and on about his rules of being a djinn). But this? This was just too much.

"Mom, you can't sell the house," she blurted out as Meg nodded her head in agreement. "I mean, seriously, we love this house. It's our house. Please tell me that it's not true."

"Oh." Her mom let out a long sigh as she sat down on the floor next them and draped her arms around them both. "I've been trying to talk to you about for the last few days, but it never seems to be the right time."

"Which means it's a sign that you shouldn't do it," Sophie pointed out. "It's the Universe's way of letting you know it's a bad idea. You should always listen to the Universe, because it knows what it's talking about."

"It's not that simple." Her mom pushed back a strand of ruler-straight hair that was identical to Sophie's own. "I love this place as much as you do—"

"Then why sell it?" Sophie pounced.

"I'm sorry, honey, but financially, it's all just getting to be too much. The mortgage is going up, and Mr. Rivers isn't sure if he can give me as many hours as I need at the store. Plus, the house needs painting, and the garden is running wild, and, well... I just can't afford to get any of it taken care of. The good news is that someone is coming to look at it tomorrow."

"This is all because I had to go to school." Meg let out a loud wail.

"What?" Her mom, who had been fanning her eyes as if to stop herself from crying, turned Meg's face toward her. "I don't understand what you mean."

"She's been hiding the mail from the real estate agents." Sophie sighed. "That's why she didn't want to go to school. Because she heard you talking about selling the house, and she was trying to stop you."

"Oh, Meggy. I'm sorry. If there was any other way I could manage, I promise you that I wouldn't be selling. Unfortunately, we don't have a choice."

"No, that's not true. There's always a choice," Sophie insisted as her cheeks start to flame with heat. "You could just ring them up and tell them that you've changed your mind. We don't need to paint the house, and I like the garden looking wild. Oh, and perhaps if we don't eat as much or buy as much stuff, then we'll have more money."

"Sophie, Meg isn't the only one who has been hiding mail. I've got a drawer full of letters from the bank."

Sophie's throat felt dry. "W-where would we go? Will we have to move to an apartment or something?"

For a moment their mom studied her hands before finally looking up, her voice sounding unnaturally bright.

"Luckily, Grandma wants us to move to Montana. The house prices are a lot cheaper there, and she's already helped line up a job for me, which means that there won't be so much financial pressure. And I've got to admit that it will be nice to have some help looking after you girls."

"No." Sophie's voice was a little above a whisper as she felt her heart pound against her chest. "Mom, please, we can't. You know what Granny thinks of Dad. She thinks that he just left us. That he is never coming back. *You even had a fight with her about it.* We can't do it. We need to stay here and wait for him. How can you give up hope on him?"

For a moment her mom didn't answer as she tightened her jaw and took a deep breath. "Sophie, I know how much you miss him... how much we all miss him, and no one wants him to come back more than I do. But wishful thinking isn't going to pay the bills. Besides, rather than getting all sad about it, perhaps we can think of it as a fresh start," she added in an overly bright voice.

"But I don't want a fresh start. I like my start just the way it is," Meg wailed, but Sophie just looked at their mom in horror as she realized that the situation had just gone from bad to worse. However, before she could say anything else, her mom got to her feet and smoothed down her jeans.

"I'm sorry, girls, but the people are coming tomorrow to look, and I'm afraid that's the end of the story. Now I want both of you to go and tidy up your rooms before dinner," she said, and then without another word she headed for the kitchen.

"We've got to stop this," Sophie announced the minute their mom had left.

"I know." Meg sniffed. "There's no way I can go to another school. One school is bad enough."

"Don't worry, Meggy." Sophie shook her head as she realized her mistake. She had been so busy freaking out that she had forgotten the most obvious thing of all. She was now a djinn, with magical powers. And combined with that, she was a positive person, and it was a well-known fact that positive djinns with magical powers didn't go to live in Montana. "It's not going to happen because I've got a plan."

"You do?" Meg perked up. "I had one as well, but then I couldn't figure out how to get the sharks into the bathtub."

"Well, my plan doesn't require any sharks at all," Sophie assured her. "And even better, I can guarantee that it will work."

It *had* to work. Besides, if you asked her, leaving the house was like admitting that her dad wasn't coming back. *It was like her mom was admitting that he wasn't coming back.* For a moment Sophie felt like crying, but she forced the tears away. She didn't care what her mom thought, she knew that they had to stay here, which was why she would do whatever it took to make it happen. Fast.

15

"MALIK, I REALLY NEED YOU TO—" SOPHIE STARTED to say as she raced into her bedroom and looked over to where the ghostly djinn was still sitting at her computer. However, the rest of the words died on her lips as she came to a halt and stared around her. Nearly every piece of clothing she owned had been pulled out of the closet; all of her board games and books were upended in one big gigantic mess; and all of it was covered in a layer of what looked like Cheetos dust. "What on earth happened here?"

"Oh." Malik blinked as he glanced around at the sea of mess that had once been her room before he finally just shrugged his shoulders. "I thought I saw a cockroach, and I kind of freaked out. I mean, those things can live without their heads attached for up to nine days. There can't be anything good about that. But don't worry, turns out it was just a piece of fluff. Talk about a close call."

"Rrr-ight." Sophie glared at him for a moment before remembering what had just happened downstairs.

"Anyway, we can talk about the mess later, but right now I need your help. What's the best sort of magic for me to use in order to stop my mom from selling the house and also to conjure up lots of money so that we're filthy rich?"

"How about the kind that you do once your djinn ring is cleansed and you've learned how to control your powers?" Malik said. "And now that we've finished talking about you, let's get back to me. Because I've had the best day ever. I've discovered this most amazing phenomenon. It's called *American Idol*. It's this place where people go and sing, and sometimes they are bad. Really, really bad, but thankfully these other people tell them to stop."

Sophie paused for a minute and stared at Malik before leaning into the computer and realizing that he was indeed watching an old *American Idol* clip on YouTube (Carrie Underwood, by the looks of it). Then she blinked and refocused.

"Okay," she finally said. "I'm going to pretend that we didn't just have that conversation, because right now I have something a bit more important to worry about. So are you going to tell me how to do it or not?"

"Not," Malik instantly answered. "I thought we'd been through this. Honestly, if I knew how often I was going to have to repeat myself, I would've bought a parrot from Rufus the Furious."

"Unless it's an emergency," Sophie reminded him as she began to cross the bedroom floor, carefully weaving her way around a Monopoly board that was lying at a crooked angle on her Twister mat. "Trust me this is an emergency of the most epic proportions. I mean, no one moves to Montana. It's just wrong. Not to mention the fact that we have to stay here for when my dad comes home."

"Do you really think he will?" Malik asked in a casual voice. "I heard your grandmother speaking to your mom the other day, and she was of the opinion that—"

"He's definitely coming back," Sophie snapped. "And we're going to be here when he does. Anyway, didn't you tell me that I was better at this magic stuff than loads of other new djinns?"

"Yes, your power is quite extraordinary, but it's still not possible to do what you want to do. I really wish you would start listening to me," he said, but Sophie hardly heard as a stabbing pain erupted in her stomach.

She doubled over and clutched at her belly as a wave of nausea overtook her while Malik's words repeated in her ear over and over again. Finally, the pain subsided, and she looked up to where Malik was watching her with interest.

"What was that all about?" he wanted to know.

"I've got no idea, but I hope it doesn't happen again." She shuddered as she rubbed her ears to get rid of Malik's voice in her head. "It's one thing to get a sore stomach, but quite another to have your every word echoing in my head."

"Hmmmm. Interesting." Malik picked up a large

leather-bound book from next to the computer, and he started to flick through it. "Describe the pain."

"Painful," she retorted. "And what's that book?"

"Oh, this big, enormous thing?" He held it up and shrugged. "I ordered it from Rufus the Furious. He's an expert on djinn training. He's forgotten more stuff than most of us know. Anyway, I thought it would help with your development. Now, would you describe the pain as shooting or continuous? Oh, and did it make you feel like throwing up?"

"Stabbing," Sophie confirmed. "And a big yes on the throwing up."

Malik was silent for a moment as he studied the book. Then he looked up in surprise. "Huh. Well, I did not see that one coming."

"See what coming?" Sophie looked at him in alarm. "What's going on?"

"Hang on a moment because I just need to check something out. I wish I had some Cheetos. Oh, and some Diet Coke as well."

"Malik, this is hardly the time to—" But the rest of Sophie's words were cut off as she once again doubled over in pain. At least there were no voices echoing in her head this time, but when she finally straightened, she saw that Malik had put the book aside and was busy eating Cheetos and gulping down some Diet Coke. And did she mention that a moment earlier there hadn't been any Cheetos or Diet Coke in the room?

"W-what's going on?" Sophie wrinkled her brow in confusion. "I thought you said you couldn't do magic anymore?"

"I didn't do it," he assured her. "You did. I just had to test to see if it worked. Plus, I was getting a little bit peckish."

"Er, no, I didn't. I mean, I think I would remember if I wished for something," she retorted while deciding that Malik had definitely been living in a bottle for too long and it had made him crazy. Unless, of course, he had been crazy before he got stuck in the bottle. That was a definite possibility.

He shook his brown hair. "Let me explain. I wished for it, and you granted it. Remember I talked about how there can be side effects to using too much magic before you can control it?"

"Side effects? You said my elbows might get itchy. This is hardly an itchy elbow." Sophie gasped before a nasty feeling came over her. "S-so what are you saying?"

"I'm saying that you have RWD. It stands for—"

"Random Wish Disorder," Sophie interrupted, and then blinked in surprise.

"Yes," Malik agreed, equally surprised. "How did you know that?"

"Um, I've got no idea," she admitted as she rubbed her chin. "It just popped into my head. Maybe I saw it in some of Harvey's research notes? He's got enough of them. What is it, anyway?"

"Basically, RWD means that if anyone wishes for something within your hearing, then you will grant it. Whether you want to or not."

"What?" Sophie looked at him in horror, but Malik didn't seem to notice.

"You know it really is quite extraordinary. According to Rufus's book, there have only been ten other cases of it over the years. Though, ironically enough it's actually those ten isolated cases of RWD that most humans seem to base their knowledge of djinns on. I mean, seriously, why on earth would djinns go around granting wishes to complete strangers if they weren't bound to them? Just shows you how dumb humans are to believe that sort of thing."

"Malik, stop rambling," Sophie yelped in alarm. "Are you trying to tell me that from now on every time someone says 'I wish' that I will grant it and get an incredibly sore stomach all at the same time? Because that's completely . . . oh, Coco Pops and Twix bars."

"Excuse me?" Malik blinked. "Is that some new sort of fancy swear the kids are saying these days, because boy oh boy, things have changed since I went into that bottle."

"No." Sophie shook her head with a sigh. "It just explains why my mom's lumpy oatmeal tasted like Coco Pops. It was because Meg wished for it, and I must've done it without even realizing. And Harvey with the Twix bar. Oh, man. How long will it last?"

"Unfortunately, Rufus really isn't very clear on that." Malik flicked through the book before picking it up and giving it a shake. Then he studied it again and finally nodded. "Here we go. Okay, so there's a very good chance that it will disappear once your djinn ring is cleansed. Though in one of the cases, it was permanent." He frowned for a moment before giving a dismissive wave of his hands. "Oh, but he was from the Shaitan tribe, so really you can't take that as gospel since not only are they a bunch of liars, but they're notoriously slow learners as well. I once tried to teach a Shaitan a Rexton curse, and I swear that I saw a palm tree grow in the amount of time it took for the silly idiot to learn it."

"But I don't finish cleansing my djinn ring until Monday night. That's four whole days away. And what about me? Does this mean that I can't do any wishing of my own?"

"That's correct." He nodded, and Sophie shot him a horrified look as she quickly closed her eyes and wished for a new Neanderthal Joe CD. She opened her eyes to discover that nothing had happened. Oh, this was not good.

"But what about my mom? I need to stop her from selling the house and also to make loads of money so that we don't go broke."

"I've already told you that even if you didn't have RWD, you still wouldn't have had the ability to manage that. I mean, I probably could've done it in my day, but you have to remember that I was a highly talented senior djinn with exceptional abilities and a real flair for creative magical interpretation, but for someone at your level, it wouldn't have worked."

"And that's meant to make me feel better?" Sophie started to fan her face. "How am I meant to stop my mom without magic?"

"Well, I don't mean to alarm you, but right now your biggest worry is how to avoid randomly granting other people their wishes," Malik informed her as he patted the book. "Because trust me, reading about some of the things that happened to these poor devils really makes me think that you're going to have an uncomfortable few days in front of you. And don't go pulling faces at me, because it's not like I didn't warn you to be careful."

"Well, you should've warned me more." Sophie stuck out her lower lip in a mulish frown. "Because I'm sure that if I knew this would happen, I would've taken it a bit more seriously."

"Did I not just mention that RWD is a very rare phenomenon?" Malik looked offended. "So how in all things shiny do you think I could've warned you? In fact, if anything, you should feel quite special—oh and look, is that the time? I really need to dash."

"Oh, no, you don't." Sophie shook her head. "You need to stay here and help me figure this out."

"Yes, but the RWD isn't fixable, and your second problem sounds like a human thing to me, and that's really not my specialty. I once tried to help this guy who had a fight with his girlfriend, and I accidently ended up turning the pair of them into cougars. Let's just say that I learned my lesson. In fact, you should write that down. Rule number one about being a djinn. If you screw up, always look for the life lesson."

Sophie glared at him for a moment, but before she could say anything, her door suddenly pushed open.

"Meg, privacy—" she started to say before looking over to see her mom standing in the doorway. Oh. She glanced over at Malik and felt the sweat bead up on her forehead. She knew that her mom couldn't see him, but it didn't make her feel any less nervous. Especially since he was now peering at her mom with interest. And was he waving at her? Sophie licked her lips. "M-mom, is something the matter?"

"I was just coming to tell you that—" her mom started to say before she suddenly paused and glanced around the room. "Sophie Charlotte-Marie Campbell, I cannot believe what I'm seeing. Look at this mess."

"Oh." Sophie gulped as she realized her mom was looking at the mess and not the ghost who was currently lifting his eyebrows in appreciation at her. "I was, er, um—"

"You were what?" her mom demanded as she folded her arms in front of her chest. "Trying to scare off the viewers when they come around tomorrow?"

"What? No." Well, yes, she did want to put the viewers off, but that wasn't why the room was messy. However, her mom didn't even seem to notice Sophie's confusion.

"Look, I know you're upset about the news, but I honestly expected more of you. Stop talking to whoever you were talking to on Skype and get this room cleaned up. Now."

Then without another word she turned and walked out of the room. Sophie wiped her brow and was pleased her mom hadn't noticed that the Skype headset wasn't even plugged into her computer and that the only person she had been talking to was Malik. And speaking of which, she turned to him and narrowed her eyes.

"Okay, so you do realize that was your fault, don't you? And what's all of the waving and eyebrow lifting about?"

"She was just looking stressed." Malik shrugged. "I thought she could use some cheering up."

"Except she couldn't even see you," Sophie reminded him. "And now you can clean up while I try to figure out a way to stop her from selling the house and stop myself from doing anymore RWD."

"Why do I have to clean it up?" Malik pouted. "I thought I explained about the cockroach. You can't blame me for that."

"Yes, well, strangely enough, I can't exactly tell my mom that the ghost djinn who has been using my computer all day thought that he saw an imaginary cockroach, so you're just going to have to suck it up and... *oh, that's it!*"

"What?" Malik yelped in alarm as he disappeared from sight and instead called out with a disembodied voice. "Where's the cockroach? Have you killed it already?"

"Malik, there's no cockroach," Sophie snapped as Malik reappeared, carefully perched up on the computer chair so he could inspect the floor. "But I just had the best idea. I mean, my mom had no idea that you made all that mess. So if you fooled her once, you can do it again."

"You want me to pretend that I can see more cockroaches?" Malik, who had finally convinced himself that the room was bug free, now proceeded to wrinkle his nose. "Because that doesn't make any sense."

"No." Sophie gave an impatient shake of her head. "I want you to scare off prospective buyers by letting them think the place is haunted."

"And how will I do that?' Malik finally sat down on the computer chair and looked at her with interest, one leg crossed over the other.

"What do you mean how will you do that? You're a ghost, so all you need to do is some freaky ghost stuff. It will be easy."

"Hmmmm. You know that sounds really undignified to me, so I think I'm going to have to pass." Malik pulled a face as he smoothed down his too-small-for-him T-shirt.

"What?" Sophie blinked at him. "I've been turned orange, and now I keep granting random wishes—not to mention getting the crippling stomachaches—and all you're worried about is your stupid dignity? Look, we need to do whatever it takes to convince my mom not to sell the house. At least not until I've got my powers back and can figure out a way to conjure us up loads of money. So are you with me?"

"Well, I'm still not—" he started to say, but after

obviously catching Sophie's annoyed glare he held up his hands. "Okay, fine. I'm in. I'll help you convince your mom not to sell the house. But let me tell you that when it comes to you filling out my Trainer Evaluation form for the Djinn Council, you had better give me lots of gold stars."

"Malik, I promise. You can have as many gold stars as you like, just as long as you help me out here."

"Fine," he muttered as he pulled another bag of Cheetos out of his pocket and muttered something about Ryan Seacrest not having to do anything dumb like this. But Sophie ignored him as she started to scoop up the mounds of clothing on the floor and shove them into the closet. Right now Ryan Seacrest was the least of her problems.

16

SO AREN'T YOU EVEN A LITTLE BIT FREAKED OUT?" Harvey asked the next morning as their homeroom teacher called the roll.

"Of course. I mean, who wants to move to Montana?" Sophie whispered back. "It's the worst thing ever. But hopefully Malik does his job."

"Do you really think he will?" Kara asked from the other side as she pulled out her sketch pad and started to draw a picture of Malik in a rapid-fire motion, as was her habit when she was worried. "It's just, I get the feeling that he's a bit"—she paused for a moment as if searching for the polite way of calling him a lunatic—"a bit...unstable," she finally finished with an inadequate wave of her hand.

"And that's just his good points," Sophie agreed. "But the way I figure it, he's also an accident waiting to happen, so hopefully he will scare the stuffing out of the people even if he doesn't mean to."

"Actually." Harvey coughed. "I wasn't talking about Malik, I was talking about you and this RWD. I mean, aren't you freaking out that your magic has gone all wonky?"

"Oh, right." Sophie nodded. To be honest, she had spent most of last night freaking out about it, before reminding herself that positive thinkers didn't freak out, they positive thought it out. After that she had been a lot better (okay, so there had been one more minor tantrum, but she had dealt with it, all right). "The thing is," she explained, "not only did I stand on my head for two hours last night, but I also totally nailed my chanting, cleansed my djinn ring, and most importantly I came up with a foolproof plan to avoid hearing anyone say 'I wish.' So as long as Malik comes through with all the poltergeist stuff, I should be fine to hold out until this is all over."

"You did? What is it?" Harvey demanded, "because I've been searching all night for some kind of solution, and I haven't found anything."

"Neanderthal Joe." Sophie grinned as she held up her iPod for a moment and then tapped at the small earphones that were hidden away behind her blond hair.

"But you're not supposed to listen to music during class." Kara looked worried.

"Yes, and I'm not supposed to randomly grant wishes to anyone who asks for them," Sophie retorted. "Besides, it's such a perfect plan."

But before she could turn on her iPod, Mr. Collins, her homeroom teacher, came up and pointed to it. "You know you can't bring those things to school. Now hand it over. You can collect it from me this afternoon. Class, I know it's Friday, and you're all excited about the weekend, but I really wish you would all zip your lips together for two minutes and listen," he said, and, as Sophie doubled over in pain, she realized that perhaps she hadn't really thought this through properly.

"Okay, so that wasn't so bad," Kara said in a bright voice at the end of the day.

"What?" Sophie widened her eyes as the bus rumbled to a halt and they scrambled off. "Not only did I have my iPod confiscated, but our entire homeroom almost ended up in *The Guinness Book of Middle School Freaks.* How's that not so bad?"

"Yes, but it only lasted for two minutes," Kara reasoned. "And when you think about it, it was a lot easier to listen when no one was talking, so really you were doing us all a favor."

"And the Britney Spears CD that I made randomly appear just because someone behind me in the cafeteria wished for it? How was that a favor?"

"I'm sure that Cheryl Robson was more than happy with it." Harvey chimed in before sighing. "But yeah, I see your point. It's a bit of a land mine. Is there anything you can do to speed up the process of cleansing the ring?"

Sophie shook her head. "I don't think so. I can't actually read Malik's book because it's in some crazy language, but I made him check it thoroughly. According to him, until Monday night, it's Sophie the Random Wish Disorder Djinn at your service."

"It's not all bad," Kara reminded her. "At least it's the weekend now, so you've got a couple of days to come up with a new plan."

"Actually," Sophie said as they came to a halt at the bottom of her path, "I've already figured it out. I mean, the whole problem with this RWD thing is that if anyone says 'I wish,' I grant it."

"Well, yeah." Harvey blinked. "But that's not exactly fresh news."

"I know, but since I can't use my iPod at school anymore, then the next best way to avoid hearing what people say is to just not be around them. I'll be fine over the weekend, but there's no way I will be able to go to school on Monday. I'm just going to have to convince my mom to let me stay home until my djinn ring is cleansed and everything is back to normal."

"Except aren't you forgetting that your mom isn't a fan of sick days?" Harvey reminded her.

"I know," Sophie agreed. "But yesterday she was so worried about me that she was almost begging me to stay at home. So I'm sure if I put the groundwork in today and then act sick all weekend, by Monday I won't have anything to worry about."

"Well, I think it sounds like a perfect plan,' Kara said in a kindhearted voice before insisting that Sophie IM them as soon as she had spoken to her mom. Once Sophie promised (three times), she waved good-bye to her friends and hurried inside while trying to get herself into sick mode. Which, considering how awful her day had been, wasn't actually that hard to do.

"Hey," she said in a feeble voice as she let out a loud cough and closed the door behind her. There was no sign of Meg under the couch today, but her mom was over in the bay window, with her laptop perched on her knee. The minute Sophie walked in, her mom shut down the computer and looked up.

"Hey to you, too. How was school?"

"Actually, not so great." Sophie coughed some more and clutched at her stomach. Would a limp be overdoing it? "I think I might have to stay home from school on Monday." And possibly Tuesday, just to catch up on all the homework she kept forgetting to do.

"Really?" Her mom folded her arms as a frown marched across her face. "And does this have anything to do with the fact that Mr. Collins called me this afternoon and said he was concerned with some of your behavior over the last couple of days?"

"What?" Sophie blinked, since she had been expecting more on the sympathy and less on the frowning. "But that's crazy. All I did was have an iPod in homeroom." *And zipped everyone's lips together, but that was beside the point since no one seemed really to realize what had happened.*

"Apparently, there have been a few incidents with your Spanish teacher as well. Mr. Collins thought it would be better to call me right away so we can nip it in the bud."

"Nip what in the bud? I'm fine," Sophie protested before remembering that she was actually sick. She coughed. "Well, I'm not fine, fine. I'm sick, but apart from being sick I'm fine. If you know what I mean."

"MG was worried you might say that."

Sophie blinked some more. "Who is MG?"

"She's one of my new online friends. I had been going onto the 'Single Moms Band Together' Web site, but after you and Meg complained about the brownie recipe, I thought I'd give Facebook a try. It's lots of fun; plus, everyone there is so supportive."

"You have a Facebook account?" Sophie was momentarily distracted as she made her way over to where her mom was sitting and peered over her shoulder to see a photograph of a woman about her mom's age with dark hair and an overly bright smile. It was obviously MG.

"Of course. You didn't think it was just for kids, did you?"

"I don't want to think about it, period." She shuddered. Seriously, she had been through a lot of weird stuff in the last five days, but this definitely had to take the cake. However, she finally remembered that right now she didn't have time in her schedule to get freaked out over her mom talking to strange women called MG on Facebook, she had too many other problems. First up, ensuring that she didn't go to school on Monday. Second, making sure that her mom didn't sell the house until after Sophie got her powers back so she could zap them up some more money.

"So anyway," her mom continued, oblivious to Sophie's

problems, "MG explained that in order for you to try to make me feel guilty about my decision to sell the house, you might act out at school and at home."

"What? That's crazy," Sophie protested. And completely untrue, since the real reason she was pretending to be sick was because she didn't want anyone to know that she was a djinn who was stuck with a temporary case of RWD. So take that, MG! *And what sort of name was MG anyway?*

"Is it?" Her mom lifted an eyebrow. "Because even if Mr. Collins hadn't called me, I've still noticed that you've been acting strangely at home. You've been secretive and edgy, not to mention the mess you made in your room yesterday. Do you have an explanation for that?"

Yes, and a very good one as well. Unfortunately, it wasn't one that she could tell her mom about. Instead, she just shook her head. "Honestly, there's nothing going on. You've got it all wrong."

"Really?" Her mom didn't look convinced. "So how come you haven't asked me how the showing went today then? I've just been speaking to the real estate agent."

"So what happened? H-how did it go?" Sophie gulped as she realized she had been so busy trying to avoid granting wishes for people that she had completely forgotten about the showing. She shot her mom a cautious glance.

"It went very well. Apparently, the people thought it seemed like a perfect family home."

"Oh." Sophie's face dropped.

"You look disappointed. What were you expecting them to say? That there was a weird smell in the basement and they got a creepy feeling about the place?"

Yes. Sophie shrugged. *That was exactly the sort of thing she had been hoping for.*

"Look, Sophie, I know you like to believe in positive thinking and signs, so don't you think this might mean that we're actually meant to sell the place?" her mom continued in a soft voice as she reached over and gave Sophie's hand a gentle squeeze.

"Of course it doesn't mean that." Sophie gave an adamant shake of her head. *As far as she could tell, the only thing it meant was that Malik was the worst djinn ghost imaginable. After all, how hard was it to haunt one measly house?*

"Well, I'm afraid it must, because the people are coming back on Monday for another look," her mom continued. "And I really wish that—"

Oh, no. Sophie stared at her mom in horror as she realized that she was about to wish for something, and that no good could come from it. She immediately clamped her hands over her ears and started to sing, "La la la la la la," to help drone out the words.

"And what was that for?" Her mom was starting to look a bit little annoyed now, but at least it had distracted her from finishing her sentence.

"Sorry." Sophie gulped while metaphorically wiping her brow in relief. "Er, it's Neanderthal Joe's new song. I guess it just got stuck in my head."

"Really?" Her mom didn't look convinced, but thankfully at that moment Meg came running into the room and demanded to know if she and Mr. Jaws could watch a shark documentary on cable. Sophie took the opportunity to hurry upstairs.

She just needed to have some peace and quiet in her room so that she could figure out a new plan, since it was fair to say that her last plan was officially screwed up. Instead, she walked into her room and saw Malik sitting at her computer wearing a PAULA WILL ALWAYS BE MY IDOL T-shirt and eating some of Meg's Halloween candy from last year.

"Hey, dog, what's up?" Malik demanded as he made a Randy Jackson–style hand move. Sophie didn't feel she could comment. On any of it.

"I'll tell you what's up," she said instead. "My mom just told me that the people are coming back to look at the house again on Monday."

"She said that?" Malik looked surprised.

"Yes, and you know what else she said?"

"What?" Malik looked at her with interest.

"Nothing," Sophie retorted. "As in, there was no mention of anything unusual about the house during their showing. In fact, it almost sounded like it was ghost free."

"Or, perhaps they were just too dense to notice my subtle approach?" he pondered as Sophie glanced at his harem pants. These were pink with some bright green trim, and they clashed violently with his Paula Abdul T-shirt. Sophie had problems believing that Malik had ever been subtle in his life.

"Or too busy watching *American Idol* on YouTube," she said instead as she reluctantly grabbed a pillow from the bed and went over to the wall. "Please, Malik, you have to promise me that you'll do something majorly big to scare them off on Monday."

"Yes, but—"

"No *yesbuts*." Sophie shook her head. "If these people like the house, then they might buy it before my djinn ring is cleansed and my powers are back to normal, and then it will be too late. I mean, what's the point of being a djinn if I'm living in Montana?"

"You know one of the *Idol* contestants was from Montana, and it really didn't look that bad... okay, fine. No Montana. I'll try my best."

"Thank you," Sophie said as she got down on her knees. "And now if you don't mind, I need to stand on my head and practice my exercises. If you could go away and do whatever it is you do, that would be great."

For a moment Malik looked like he was going to say something before he finally clicked his fingers and disappeared from sight. Then Sophie balanced on her head and started to chant the words he had given her, while thinking positive, happy thoughts. After all, as a very positive person, she had no doubt that everything would be fine. It *had* to be.

17

"SO NO SICK DAY, HUH?" HARVEY ASKED ON MONDAY morning as they all piled off the bus and made their way into the main entrance. Fall had really started to make its presence felt, and it was far too cool to sit out on the boulder, so they headed straight for their lockers.

"No." Sophie shook her head since despite coughing (and limping) all weekend, her mom had refused point blank to let Sophie stay home. Which in itself wouldn't have been so bad if every second sentence that her mom had uttered hadn't been accompanied by the words *"MG said."* Even Meg was so sick of hearing it she'd said that unless MG knew the difference between a great white and a tiger shark, then she wasn't interested.

Not that her mom had even seemed bothered. Instead, she spent the entire weekend either on the computer or cleaning up the yard before the people came back for a second showing. Meanwhile, Sophie practically had to tie Malik down to give him a few lessons in the art of scaring people. She had made him sit through some select choices from Harvey's scary movie collection to give him a few clues, and Kara had shown him how to use tomato ketchup to write on the walls. In the end they had decided to keep it simple and have him do something like "Beware" and "Doomed."

"Still," Kara piped in, "you didn't have any accidents over the weekend, so you just need to get through today and—"

But Sophie hardly heard the rest of her friend's sentence as she caught sight of Jonathan Tait walking toward them. Without a word she darted behind the nearest locker (but not before noticing how gorgeous he looked in dark denims, a blue retro Adidas T-shirt, and some new sneakers with yellow laces).

"Hey, Jonathan," she heard Kara say. "Sophie is… er, well, she was here a minute ago." As Kara spoke she glanced around before catching sight of Sophie crouched behind the locker. Her friend widened her eyes at her, but Sophie just shook her head and made the international sign for Don't tell him that I'm here or I will die.

"Oh," Jonathan said in his gorgeous voice, which made Sophie go all tingly. "Well, can you tell her that I'm looking for her? I've got something to give her."

"O-of course." Kara nodded while shooting Sophie another pleading glance. Sophie immediately narrowed her eyes and gave three quick shakes of her head.

"Okay, great. So I guess I'll see you guys around then."

Jonathan shrugged as he gave Kara and Harvey a friendly smile and then loped off in the other direction.

"Um, so according to his body language, I'm pretty sure he likes you, and since you have talked nonstop about him since you were seven years old, I can't quite figure out why you're avoiding him?" Harvey joined Sophie in her crouching position beside the locker as she peered down the corridor to make sure Jonathan was gone.

"Yes, but right now I'm like a walking time bomb. So I figured that the best thing to do was just stay out of his way today, and then tomorrow when I've finished cleansing my djinn ring and the RWD has gone away, things can be back to normal. Well, as normal as it can be considering that I'm a djinn," Sophie explained. After all, it was one thing for his sister to think she was a freak, but it was another thing entirely for Jonathan to think it.

"So that's your plan? To hide out every time you see Jonathan Tait?" Harvey raised an eyebrow.

"Pretty much." Sophie nodded. "Oh, and I've also decided that if anyone tries to say 'I wish' around me, I'll just hum in my head and drown out the words."

Harvey's eyebrow raised even higher, but before he could comment Kara cut in and shot Sophie a supportive smile.

"Well, I think that's an excellent idea, and besides, it won't be long before this is all over and Sophie can talk to Jonathan again without risking anything going weird."

"Thanks, K." Sophie returned the smile, and then, once the coast was Jonathan Tait clear, they all hurried to assembly. Sophie tried to ignore the fact that this time last week she had been full of hope and excitement about starting sixth grade. It had been a long seven days, that was for sure. She noticed Mr. Collins was looking at her intently, and she only just revisited the urge to poke her tongue at him since his phone call to her mom was the whole reason she was stuck at school now instead of in the safety of her own room.

Still, she was a positive person, and she had figured out that she had only twelve hours until the ring was cleansed and the RWD was gone. She glanced at her watch. Actually, make that eleven hours and thirty-two minutes. Next to her Kara reached over and gave Sophie's hand a comforting squeeze as Principal Gerrard tapped the microphone.

Sophie felt herself start to relax. Everything was going to be okay. She just needed to stay calm, focus her thoughts, and really—

"Right. Robert Robertson Middle School, I really wish that—"

Oh, no. It was the zipped lips all over again, and for a moment Sophie froze in alarm before she quickly thrust her hands over her ears and started to hum "Zombie Vegas" silently in her mind to block out the words. She could do it. She was not listening. She could not hear. She... hey, it was working! Sophie blinked as she realized that her stomach wasn't hurting. That was so cool. She'd avoided granting an "I wish" wish.

"Nice work." Kara mouthed from next to her while Harvey gave her a thumbs-up. Suddenly, Sophie felt some of her good mood return. *See, all she needed to do was keep her positive attitude.*

By the end of the day Sophie had hummed her way through four songs, and, according to Kara, she had avoided conjuring up some blueberry muffins, a set of false nails, and in Melissa Tait's case, a Jessica Alba nose. She had also managed to avoid getting a detention from Señor Rena by frantically doing her homework while they were cooped up in the janitor's closet during their lunch break. But most importantly, she had ducked and hidden herself away from Jonathan Tait no fewer than five times. Of course, the irony wasn't lost on her that last week her greatest wish would've been to know that Jonathan was looking for her in the first place.

"Are you sure this is really necessary?" Harvey double-checked as they lurked by the boulder in front of the school that afternoon. Normally, they just went straight over and joined the bus line, but Sophie had decided that it was too risky and that it was better to wait separately and then just race over when their bus arrived.

"I'm sure," she said in a confident voice. In fact, if the government ever wanted to hire specially trained djinn secret agents, perhaps they would recruit her, since she was turning out to be quite good at this covert stuff. Then she glanced at her watch. "I only have six hours left before this whole RWD thing will be over and everything will be fine."

"Okay, if you . . . shoot," Kara cried out as she looked at her empty hands. "I've left my portfolio in the art room, and I promised Mrs. Ryder I would work on my watercolors tonight. I'll have to go back and get it."

Sophie and Harvey looked at each other in alarm before Harvey gave a polite cough.

"I'll go with you," he told her.

"I think I can go to the art room on my own," Kara retorted.

"Okay, so how about we use your recent visit to the art supply store on Hamilton as an example?" Harvey suggested in a polite voice. "I do believe your exact words were 'I'll just go get some charcoal and then I'll meet you both in Mickey D's in five minutes.' Two hours and three Big Macs later and Sophie and I had to send out a search party."

"And even then you didn't come willingly." Sophie shot Kara an apologetic grin. "You're worse than Meg when she goes to the aquarium. Anyway, you guys go and get the portfolio, and I'll make sure that the bus doesn't leave without you."

"We won't be long," Harvey promised as he started to jog slowly back to the main building, Kara trailing in his wake. Sophie waited until her friends had disappeared before she wrapped her jacket closer around her and leaned against the boulder. In half an hour she would be safely back at home and—

"Sophie, there you are," a voice said from behind, and Sophie felt the hairs on the back of her neck start to prickle as she slowly turned around to see Jonathan Tait standing in front of her. "I've been looking for you all day."

"You have?" Sophie gulped as she realized she might have to withdraw her application to the Secret Service.

"Yeah, didn't you see me near the vending machines? I was waving at you?" he asked, his blue eyes full of confusion.

"R-really?" she stammered instead. "I didn't realize. My mom is thinking of getting my eyes checked because my vision's so bad."

"Oh." He nodded as he ran a hand through his golden curls. "I was starting to get worried that you were avoiding me because of how mental Melissa went on you."

"What?" She looked at him blankly for a moment before she realized that Jonathan was actually waiting for her to speak. "I mean, no, it's definitely not like that. Melissa who? That's what I say."

"Well, that's good to know." He suddenly grinned as he pulled a CD out of his bag. "Anyway, I wanted to give you this. It's the set list for the concert."

"Thanks." Sophie reached out to take the CD and felt

a little bubble of happiness go racing through her as his finger grazed hers. "And hey, I'm sorry you couldn't find me today. I-it's been a bit of a crazy time lately, but I'm pretty certain that things will be back to normal tomorrow. In fact, I can almost guarantee it."

"Really?" He didn't pull his hand away, and Sophie felt herself getting lost in his gorgeous eyes.

"Really," she agreed in a croaky voice as she continued to stare at his perfect face.

"Well, that's good. But you know, if there is something weird going on, I wish you'd tell me what it is."

Unfortunately, Sophie was so caught up in the sensation of being close to Jonathan Tait that it wasn't until the first stab of pain hit her stomach that she quite realized what he had just said.

Nooooooooooooooooooo she wanted to scream out loud, but of course between the pain and the overwhelming desire to speak, that just wasn't possible.

"Are you okay?" Jonathan looked at her concern.

"Well, my stomach hurts," she admitted as she managed to stand up straight again. "But it's only because I've got this thing called Random Wish Disorder, or RWD, as they say in the business."

What? No. Shut up, a tiny voice at the back of her head tried to scream out, but another part of her brain ignored it by humming a Neanderthal Joe song. *Oh, that was just plain evil.*

"What?" Jonathan looked even more perplexed. "I don't think I get what you're talking about."

"Sorry." She shot him a goofy look as her inner voice was completely drowned out. "I'm not explaining this very well. I should probably start at the beginning. You see, last week while I was staring at you through Mr. Rivers's basement window I accidently released a djinn called Malik, who in turn convinced me to wear his djinn ring. See, isn't it pretty? Anyway, now I'm a djinn, and not only did I magically conjure up the Neanderthal Joe tickets, but now every time someone says the words 'I wish,' I'm compelled to do it, and—"

Before she could say anything else, Harvey and Kara suddenly reappeared. After taking one look at the situation, Harvey clamped his hand firmly over Sophie's mouth so that the rest of her words sounded muffled. Not that it really mattered, since after staring at her like she was something that Mr. Jaws had dragged in from the garden, Jonathan turned and walked in the other direction without even a backward glance. As he disappeared from sight, Sophie was fairly certain that she now had another contender for worst day ever.

18

DON'T." SOPHIE SHOOK HER HEAD AS THEY REACHed the bottom of her path.

"I was only going to tell you that it probably isn't as bad as you think," Kara protested in a hopeful voice.

"I know, but don't. Because, trust me, I was there. I know how bad it was," Sophie assured her. "Anyway, I promise that I'll call you guys later, but right now I just want to go crawl into a deep, dark hole."

"But—" Kara started to say before Harvey reached for her arm.

"Come on, Kara. Just give her some time."

Sophie shot them both a grateful glance and slowly made her way up the path while trying not to think of the disaster that was her life. Her mom's car was parked in the driveway. For a moment she paused, since her mom normally worked later on Mondays and it was Sophie's job to pick up Meg from the Daltons and keep an eye on her.

Still, this was probably better; the only thing she wanted to keep an eye on was the underside of her comforter, once she buried herself in it.

She pushed open the door and was just heading for the stairs when her mom poked her head out of the kitchen.

"There you are. Can you come in here for a minute? There's something I need to talk to you about."

Sophie looked longingly at the stairs. All she wanted to do was go upstairs and hide away for the next hundred years or so, but unfortunately, judging by the "I'm the parent in this family" look that her mom had going on, saying no wasn't really an option. She walked into the kitchen and looked over to where Meg was sitting at the table with a bowl of Coco Pops in front of her, looking gloomy. Okay, so that couldn't be good since despite her sister's continued pleas, Coco Pops weren't something that even made it onto the shopping list. Which meant—

Sophie felt the blood drain away from her face.

"You've sold the house, haven't you?"

"I'm sorry, honey. I know it's not what you want, but the people made us an offer this afternoon. A good offer. I just need to sign the papers, and it will all be done."

"Mom, you—"

"Please, Sophie. Don't make this harder than it has to be. I've already told you that we need the money, but it's actually your erratic behavior that has helped me to decide that perhaps a move would be a good thing. I don't understand what's gotten into you lately, but I know that it can't go on. When we're in Montana, I'll have the support of my parents, and perhaps you'll feel a bit more settled and secure."

"Mom, no. If this is something that stupid MG said—"

"Sophie, that's enough," her mom cut her off in a cool voice. "If you can't discuss this properly, then you can go to your room and come back down when you're feeling a bit more composed."

"Fine." Sophie took a deep breath and willed herself not to burst out crying, but seriously, this was just too much. "But don't expect me to be down again anytime soon."

Then without another word, she turned and raced upstairs clapping her hands as she went. Malik was already waiting for her up in her bedroom. Well, she liked to think he was, but judging by the number of Cheetos packets that were lying around, there was a strong possibility that he had been there all day. He was also wearing one of her favorite Billabong T-shirts, which looked ridiculous against his harem pants and his Zac Efron face.

"Ooh, you know that frown thing you're doing with your face is really most unattractive," Malik said the minute she stepped through the door. "You might want to stop doing that before you go to this concert of yours. You know how the old saying goes: 'No one likes a frowner.'"

"Yes, well, I guess it's lucky then that I'm not going to the concert on Saturday." Sophie glared as she stomped over to her bed and sat down on the corner of it.

"Don't tell me that the tickets you conjured up dissolved? That can happen sometimes when you're not completely focused."

"What?" Sophie looked at him in alarm since this was the first she had heard of dissolving magic. However, she reached over to her nightstand and opened the drawer to display her pristine Neanderthal Joe ticket. "Nope, it's not dissolved. I'm not going because Jonathan Tait is never going to speak to me again. And do you want to know why he's never going to speak to me again?"

"Not really." Malik quickly shook his Zac-like hair, but Sophie ignored him.

"It was because Jonathan Tait wished I would tell him what was going on."

"Ouch." Malik pulled a face.

"I'll say ouch," Sophie agreed as she narrowed her eyes. "And it gets better. Because those people now want to buy our house. As in *buy* it. This is all your fault."

"My fault?" Malik protested as he turned his face into the picture of innocence. "You should try haunting a house. I tell you, it's not as easy as it looks. All that moving from one room to another, then hoping that they're facing the right direction when you're in there acting like an idiot. Honestly, it was one disaster after another. But you can't say that I didn't try."

"Yes, but if you hadn't come along and turned me into a stupid djinn, then I wouldn't be in this stupid situation to begin with."

"Ah, but if I hadn't turned you into a djinn, then you wouldn't have been able to conjure up the Neanderthal Joe tickets."

"I wouldn't have needed to because I wouldn't have been forced to spend my life savings on some potion to stop me from looking orange," Sophie countered.

"You know a djinn could start to take offense at that." Malik sniffed. "I mean, I was kind enough to bestow upon you unlimited power and magic, but are you even a little bit grateful? I think not—"

"Bestow upon me?" Sophie narrowed her eyes. "You tricked me into it, and even worse, you had no idea if I would even live or not."

"And did you die? No." Malik stood up and brushed some crumbs off his (or should she say *her*) T-shirt. "Honestly, you're overreacting."

Sophie glared at him as she reached over to her nightstand and threw her library book at his head.

"Ouch," Malik complained; he disappeared from sight as the book went sailing straight through the air where he had just been standing before landing spine up on the floor. "You know, if I had a corporeal body, then that would've really hurt."

"Good, because I'm mad at you. In fact, unless you can think of a way to stop my mom from signing those papers, or stop Jonathan Tait from thinking that I'm a nutcase, then you can just go away. Okay?" Sophie glared at him before he finally seemed to get her message, and with barely a shrug of his shoulders, he disappeared from sight, leaving her to get on with the important job of trying to figure out a new plan.

However, by seven o'clock that night Sophie realized that there was no new plan. She was all planned out. All her positive thinking. All her looking on the bright side. And for what? So that she could have a horrible, boring future in Montana, with no Jonathan Tait and even worse, no Kara or Harvey?

No Harvey and Kara.

The thought of it made Sophie's stomach contract in panic. After all, the only thing that had stopped her from losing her mind with this whole djinn business was the fact that her two BFFs had been with her the whole way. And she didn't care what Harvey said, it wouldn't be the same if they just IMed each night. Especially since for all she knew, Montana didn't even have broadband.

Sophie pulled the comforter farther over her head while downstairs she could hear her mom and Meg talking and having dinner. Meg didn't even seem that upset anymore. Talk about a traitor. She had been bought out by a box of Coco Pops. But before Sophie could get even gloomier, there was a rustling noise on the other side of the room, and she let out a groan.

"Go away, Malik. I mean it—I'm never talking to you again."

"Wise choice," an unfamiliar voice said. "Malik always was a loose cannon who could talk a person into doing the exact thing he or she didn't want to do. And not that I'm one for holding grudges, but it will still be another few millennia before I forget about the whole Egyptian incident."

Sophie blinked as she pushed the comforter away from her face and discovered that there was a very fat orange man in a garish Hawaiian shirt sitting cross-legged in the corner of her room, hovering five feet off the ground. She felt the blood start to pound around her temples. Last time this had happened, her life had taken one big detour for the worse, and while she wasn't quite sure if there was room for any more "worse" this time, all the same she clutched at the comforter and narrowed her eyes.

"Okay, who are you, and what do you want? Because if you're here to trick me into wearing your djinn ring, then I'm afraid it's too late."

"Boy, Malik wasn't joking when he said you were a touch on the dramatic side," the orange guy said as he floated down to the ground and held a large box in his hand. "I'm actually looking for the old boy. Is he around?"

"No, he's not," Sophie retorted. "And you still haven't told me who you are."

"A thousand apologies, dear child. I'm Rufus."

"Rufus the Furious?" Sophie blinked since, despite having seen his picture on the back of the potion bottle every night when she used it, she couldn't really see the resemblance. For a start, his chin was lost in a sea of necks, and his nose was abnormally large, and (please don't judge her for this) there was something very unpleasing about his eyebrows. In fact, all Sophie could figure was that he must've used a whole lot of Photoshop on his Web site.

"Actually, I prefer Rufus the Filthy Rich. It has a much nicer ring to it. Plus, I think it presents a more positive image," he explained in a polite voice as he peered around the room with interest. "So do you know when Malik will be back?"

"Never," Sophie reminded him. "Why do you want him anyway?"

"Well, he's been buying quite a lot of stuff from the shop lately, and would you believe that on his last purchase we forgot to include the free steak knives?" He held out the box, and Sophie realized that there were indeed six gleaming steak knives in there. "Well, I say that 'we' forgot, but really it was that waste of space ifrit, whom I felt sorry enough to employ. Honestly, the number one rule of being a djinn is never to employ an ifrit to do a minion's work, but did I listen? No, I did not. Actually, you should write that down."

Sophie looked at him blankly as she tried to figure out if all djinns were as crazy as Malik and Rufus.

"Yes, well, you're going to have to find him somewhere else because I'm done with him," Sophie said with a sniff as she pretended to dust off her hands in the air. "It's over."

"Understandable." Rufus gave a sympathetic nod, which made the layers of fat around his neck wobble like a turkey's. "Since even when he was a djinn he was more than a little annoying. But as much as I hate to defend the old guy, he really has been trying to help you out. I mean, not everyone orders my limited-edition, leather-bound *Djinn Guide for the Newly Blessed Children of the Smokeless Fire.*"

"Yes, well, if he really wanted to help me out, he should've never tricked me into taking his stupid ring in the first stupid place," Sophie retorted as she picked up her pillow and started to squeeze it into a small ball. "I mean, seriously, first he could've killed me. Killed me dead. And now, thanks to this equally stupid RWD, my life is ruined. Forever—which, since I'm stuck as a stupid djinn, literally is forever. And while as a rule I try to stay positive, I'm really struggling to see how any of this is good."

"You know, it almost sounds like you don't want to be a djinn." Rufus wrinkled his orange brow in surprise.

"Really? And here I was thinking that I was hiding my feelings." Sophie rolled her eyes, still stinging with the injustice of the whole situation.

"So bear with me if I'm asking a really dumb question here, but if you don't want to be a djinn, then why are you one?" Rufus carefully put the steak knives down on her computer chair and moved over to her bookshelf, where her djinn ring cleanser was nestled next to the collection of body washes and scented moisturizers that her grandma sent her every year for Christmas.

"Because I don't have a choice in the matter," Sophie reminded him as she watched while he picked up the ring cleanser and shook the bottle. "What are you doing?"

"I'm seeing how much of this you've used. It looks like you've got one more cleanse to do."

"That's right." Sophie automatically nodded as she checked her watch. "In an hour."

"Which means it's not too late to reverse your powers. I'm surprised that Malik didn't mention it to you."

"What?" The word exploded from her mouth like a hurricane. "You cannot be serious. Malik told me that it was completely irreversible. He said the Djinn Council gets really cranky when djinns don't pass on their powers."

"Yeah, well, that's nothing compared to how they get if you don't submit your M457-B6 by the end of the fiscal year, but don't get me started on that, or we'll be here all night. Anyway, where was I?" He blinked as he pulled a large handkerchief out of his pocket and wiped down his wide orange brow.

"You were saying it wasn't too late for me to reverse this whole djinn thing. Are you serious?"

"Of course I am. I mean, yes, the council requires that a djinn pass his or her powers on, but djinns in training are required by law to have a one-week opt-out clause. All a person needs to do is take a Reversal Pill, which my store happens to sell for the 'Why don't you just rob me?' price of forty-two dollars, including pigeon delivery and a variety of flavors. Once the pill is taken, the powers will pass over to the Djinn Council, and they will hand them on to a suitable recipient."

"And what happens to me?"

"Your life goes back to the way it was. Actually, it literally goes back to the way it was, so it will be like this whole week has never happened."

Sophie felt her mouth go dry. "As in no embarrassing conversations with Jonathan Tait? No acting weirdly and freaking my mom out so much that she becomes even more adamant about selling the house than she already is?"

Rufus looked at her blankly. "I guess not. You will wake up and go back to the day you put the ring on, except this time you won't put the ring on and your life will return to normal."

Unbelievable.

Like it was 100 percent unbelievable. And more importantly, it was the answer she had been looking for. Then she narrowed her eyes and studied Rufus's face. "If all of this is true, then why on earth didn't Malik say anything?"

"Well, it's hard to tell." Rufus shrugged. "I mean, Malik hasn't always had the best memory, so it might've just slipped his mind. Of course, the more obvious reason is that if you keep his powers, then he gets to stay in noncorporeal form and hang out with everyone, but if the powers revert to the Djinn Council, then..." Rufus paused for a moment and wiped his brow for a second time.

"Then what?" Sophie demanded in an urgent voice as she glanced at her watch. Fifty-two minutes to go.

"Then nothing," Rufus told her. "Malik would simply cease to exist."

19

TWENTY-THREE MINUTES LATER, SOPHIE STARED AT the small turquoise pill that the pigeon had delivered about three seconds after Rufus the Furious had departed. According to the djinn, all she had to do was swallow it before it was time to do the final cleanse of her djinn ring, and presto! her life would return to Sunday at Mr. Rivers's house with bratty Ryan the biter. Yet despite all of this, she still hadn't taken it. Finally, Sophie clapped her hands, and a second later Malik was in front of her.

"Thank goodness you called. I've got news," he said the minute he appeared, though this time he didn't look like Zac Efron; he was now the spitting image of Eddie Henry, the bass player from Neanderthal Joe. Sophie widened her eyes, and Malik grinned. "Oh, do you like it? I've been working on it ever since you got RWD. I thought it might cheer you up a bit," he said as he did a very uncool bow that was nothing like Eddie.

Sophie felt herself giggling, but before she could answer him, Malik caught sight of the pill in her hand and his shoulders immediately dropped.

"Oh, I see you've got a Reversal Pill. Nice color. Apparently, the turquoise one tastes best."

Sophie, who hadn't quite been sure how to start the whole "You're going to die for real this time" conversation, felt a little taken aback. "You're not mad at me?"

"Eh." He shrugged. "There was a chance it would happen, and while I suppose I wish you'd taken to the whole djinn thing—especially since your powers and abilities really are quite extraordinary—I can't blame you for not wanting to do it."

"So why did you lie to me and say there was no way to reverse it?"

"What was rule number one I told you about being a djinn?" he demanded, but when Sophie scratched her head, he rolled his eyes. "Never trust another djinn. Or a djinn ghost, for that matter, because we're all liars. Anyway, how did you find out? Don't tell me that you learned how to read djinnese?" he said as he glanced over to the large leather-bound book that was still sitting on the computer table.

Sophie didn't even know there was a language called djinnese, and so she quickly shook her head.

"Rufus came around looking for you. Apparently, they forgot to send you your free steak knives with your last purchase."

"Steak knives?" Malik widened his Eddie Henry eyes in excitement as he caught sight of them. He rushed over and inspected them for a moment before letting out a low whistle. "Very nice. Oh, and look at the blade. I bet they would slice through an eye fillet like it was a...well, I suppose that doesn't matter now, but you've got to admit that, as far as steak knives go, these are good ones."

Sophie gulped as she studied the pill in her hand. This wasn't quite going as planned. "But you understand why I have to do this, right? I mean, it's not like I hate you or anything. In fact, apart from your habit of being crazy, you're sort of cool as far as djinn guides go."

"Is this going to be one of those things when you start to cry?" Malik dragged his attention away from the steak knives. "Because I do believe that I've warned you before that crying girls aren't really my specialty."

"Okay." Sophie clamped down on her tongue to stop herself from getting all sniffly. "S-so how do you want to do this thing? W-would you like one final look at YouTube? Or some Cheetos? Because I wouldn't mind."

For a moment Malik looked at the computer monitor before regretfully shaking his head. "Better not. That thing is a black hole of time, and I guess if you're going to do this, you need to do it soon. Perhaps we could just sit quietly? Oh, and if it's any consolation, I've heard it doesn't hurt much," he said in a bright voice, which was at odds with his Adam's apple, which was bobbing up and down in his neck.

Sophie's heart started to pound as she watched him sit cross-legged on the floor, still clutching at the steak knives like they were a bag of diamond-encrusted Cheetos. She went to join him, but as she did so, her elbow hit the small silver box that her dad had given her for her seventh birthday, just weeks before he disappeared.

She grabbed it before it hit the carpet and cradled it carefully in her hands as she felt her resolve thicken. Yes, it sucked, what was about to happen to Malik, but there was no way she could pass up this chance to go back to her normal life and to try again to convince her mom not to sell the house—this time without all the crazy antics to accompany her efforts.

"Where did you get that?" Malik suddenly cut into her thoughts as he stared at the box.

"What do you mean?"

"That box. Why do you have a djinn safe-deposit box in your bedroom? And more importantly, why have I never seen it before?"

"Probably because you couldn't eat it," Sophie retorted. "And why wouldn't I have it in here? My dad gave it to me for a birthday present."

"Your dad? But why would he have a—" Malik started to say before widening his eyes. "Can I see what your dad looks like?"

"Malik." Sophie looked at her watch. "I really don't... okay, fine," she relented as she caught his determined stare—the last time she had seen it was when he had nagged her to teach him how to download songs from iTunes. She reached over to a small silver-framed photo of her dad and passed it to Malik. It had been taken after a family trip to Disneyland, and even though her dad still had his goofy ears on, he looked reassuringly familiar.

"Of course!" Malik suddenly nodded his head in understanding before he began to mutter to himself. "It's so obvious. I mean, all that power she had. How did I not figure it out? Honestly, Malik, sometimes I worry about you."

"Malik? What's going on? Why are you talking to yourself like that? Are you trying to say that you know my dad?"

"Well, I wouldn't say that 'I know him,' know him. But of course I've heard of him. Who hasn't? Especially after what happened in Prussia. Tariq the Awesome is a legend."

"Tariq? My dad's name isn't Tariq, it's Terry. And how on earth could you know him when you're a djinn, and he's a—" Sophie paused for a minute and felt her head start to spin. She wasn't sure how long it took before she finally regained the power of speech. But finally, she managed to croak, "Are you telling me that my dad's a djinn?"

"Isn't that what I just said?" Malik demanded. "Honestly, Sophie, you really need to keep up."

However, Sophie hardly heard as she tried to process what Malik was saying. Her father was a djinn. Like her. Suddenly, she froze as she thought of all the stories he used to tell. And how she knew what RWD stood for.

She had grown up learning all about djinns, without even realizing it.

That's why her magic was so good. Not just because of Malik's power, but because she already had djinn blood. Like her dad. Which also meant that her dad could do magic, he could fly, and he could . . . *live forever.*

Sophie felt the blood pound in her temples as she turned back to Malik.

"If my dad's a djinn, then he must still be alive! Does that mean you know where he is?"

"Sorry." Malik shook his head. "Like I said, I don't know him personally."

"But you could ask around, right?" Sophie jumped to her feet and started to frantically look around. "I mean, one of your djinn friends might know him. They might know what has happened to him."

"Well, the best place to start is actually in that box you have." Malik nodded at it. "I mean, he probably left it for you on purpose, since those things are designed to carry everyone's deepest, darkest secrets. Plus, they are really good for hiding stolen goods and—"

"This?" Sophie cut him off as she held it up. "Are you saying that the answers to what happened to my dad could be in this thing? But it doesn't even open. It never has. Not even when Meg thought it would be funny to drop it out the window."

"That's why they're called safe-deposit boxes," Malik explained. "Because the only way they can be opened is if you take them to some dusty vault at the Djinn Council and use a specially designed key."

"Okay, then, so let's do that." Sophie eagerly nodded as the excitement started to thump through her body. "Let's do that right now. You can take me, right?"

"Actually." Malik gave a polite cough as he nodded at the turquoise pill that was now sitting on the night-stand. "In a few minutes I'm not going to exist, and you're just going to be a normal girl who will have forgotten all about this."

"What?" Sophie's hope went screeching to an abrupt halt. "Are you saying that if I'm not a djinn, then I'll never be able to get the key to this box and find out what happened to my dad?"

"I'm saying that you won't even remember what the box means. And if by a small chance you do, it won't matter anyway, since the only way you can go to the Djinn Council and open it is if you're a—"

"A djinn?" Sophie finished off in horror as Malik nodded.

"I'm afraid so. Remember I told you they were a pack of old women? Well, this is yet another example of their many stupid rules that make no sense. I'm sorry, Sophie, I wish I had better... and hey, what are you doing? That thing won't work if you crush it like that."

"I don't want it to work," Sophie informed him as she used the corner of the box to smash the pill into turquoise powder.

"Are you saying that you're not going to take it?"

"Yes, that's what I'm saying," Sophie agreed as she finished crushing the pill and then slipped off the rhinestone studded apple ring so she could cleanse it. Funny—it had caused her so much trouble, but now it might be the one thing to grant her greatest wish. Finding out where her dad had gone.

SOPHIE, MAY I COME IN?" HER MOM POKED HER head into the bedroom the following Saturday, which in turn almost caused Sophie to take her eye out with the mascara wand she had in her hand. She had been undecided whether or not to wear makeup to the concert, but after that near-fatality she decided that it must be the Universe giving her a sign to stick to lip gloss and some body glitter. She screwed the cap on and turned around to face her mom.

"Jonathan's brother is coming around to get me in ten minutes," she reminded her mom before double-checking her hair—still flat and blond and doing what it always did, more's the pity. And while she was more than a little tempted to give it a bit of a zap with her djinn magic, after everything that had happened last week, she had decided that Malik was right. Rule number one about being a djinn was knowing when to use your magic and knowing when just to use hair product. She had even written it down.

"I promise it won't take long," her mom assured her

as she walked in and sat down on the corner of the bed. "Okay, I'm not going to beat around the bush. I know you haven't been happy with me this week."

"Yes, well, just because Meg will sell her soul for a box of Coco Pops doesn't mean I will," Sophie retorted as some of her happy mood disappeared. Ever since she had cleansed her djinn ring for the final time on Monday night, her life had started to improve. Malik had helped her compose a letter to the Djinn Council to talk to them about getting the key for her dad's box, and even better, Jonathan Tait had totally believed her that her whole "I'm a djinn" speech was actually a result of having played The Sims for five hours straight. She felt bad about lying to him, but there was no way she was ready for him to know the truth about her. Especially if she was moving to Montana and was never going to see him again. Which brought her to the downside of everything, since despite all her efforts, the one thing that Sophie hadn't been able to figure was how to stop her mom from selling the house.

"I know," her mom agreed. "In fact, you've made your feelings on the matter very clear."

"So what's this about then?" Sophie sniffed before realizing that Malik's large leather-bound djinn book was next to the computer. Oh, yeah, that was the other thing she hadn't managed to fix. Malik's ability to make a mess. She casually picked up her favorite cardigan and draped it over the book.

"Well, I've been speaking to MG about the move, and—"

"What? Let me guess, MG thinks we should move tomorrow because it's stupid to wait until the end of term like you promised?" Sophie finished hiding the book and then folded her arms.

"Actually, MG thinks that perhaps I've been so busy looking for a quick fix to my problems that I was ignoring the fact that changing my location won't change what's really wrong. I mean, yes, the money is a worry, but there are other ways to earn more money, which is why I've started talking to some of the stores who used to sell my pottery. Anyway, I've managed to get a few commissions. So while I might be a bit busier after work, we should be better off. I've even spoken to the bank, and they're convinced that I can keep up my repayments."

"What?" Sophie stared at her blankly for a moment. After all, her stomach didn't hurt, so she knew it wasn't RWD, and she certainly hadn't tried to influence her mom's decision with magic (only because she didn't know how). "A-are you messing with me?"

Her mom shook her head and started to smile. I called the real estate agent today. When I signed the contract, I asked him to put in a three-day cooling-off period, and so I told him that I'd changed my mind."

But Sophie didn't hear anything else as she launched herself at her mom in a gigantic hug.

"So can you forgive me for putting you through that?" her mom asked as she finally disentangled herself.

"Can you forgive me for being so bratty?" Sophie countered. "I mean, I knew you weren't doing it on purpose, but I just couldn't imagine living anywhere but here."

"You were just doing what you believed in." Her mom gave her another hug. "And actually, never have you reminded me more of your father than at this moment."

Sophie glanced over to the small silver box that was sitting next to her bed. She longed to tell her mom everything that was going on, but she realized that right now wasn't the time. Instead, she just gulped as something else occurred to her.

Despite doing an extensive search on the Internet, Harvey never had been able to find any reference to a story about a foolish djinn and the equally foolish human girl who had fallen in love with each other. Which had gotten her thinking.

"Mom," she suddenly asked, "how did you and dad first meet?"

"At college," her mom said in surprise. "You know that."

"Yes, but I mean the first time," Sophie clarified, and she was surprised to see a small half smile on her mom's lips.

"Oh. Well, it was rather strange really. I was in this antiques store looking for a present for your grandmother. You know she likes to collect teaspoons. Anyway, I saw this bottle—it was blue and very old, and for some reason I felt really drawn to it. *Now this next bit is going to sound crazy.* Somehow, I dropped the bottle, and then, almost out of nowhere, your father appeared. Now I realize he must've walked up behind me and given me a scare, and that's how I dropped it in the first place. Well, I took one look at him and fell instantly in love. He was such a romantic, he immediately asked me to make a wish, and so—"

"You wished that he would never leave," Sophie finished off, and her mom, who had been dabbing her eyes, suddenly gave her a watery smile.

"Yes, so I guess I have told you that story already. Anyway." Her mom suddenly got to her feet, as if trying to push aside some memories. "You've got a concert to go to. I just wanted to let you know the good news before you went."

"Thanks, Mom. Really." Sophie dabbed at her own eyes, extra pleased that she hadn't bothered with the mascara, because from what she'd read, her face would now be resembling that of a panda bear. Then she shot her mom a shy smile. "And by the way, I guess I owe MG an apology. I might've said her name in vain a few times."

"You don't owe her anything. But if you like, I'll tell her you said hi." Her mom grinned. "I'm logging on with her tonight. She has a cooking problem that she wants some help with."

"Really?" Sophie looked at her in surprise since she

couldn't imagine anyone asking her mom a cooking question unless it involved the words *"charcoal"* and *"a lot."*

"Ironic, isn't it? But apparently she has this thing for Cheetos, and she wants to know if I have any recipes for her."

"Cheetos? Did you say Cheetos?"

"I know, weird. I did find one recipe where you can crush them and then use them to coat chicken, but between you and me, I can't imagine it tasting any good."

But Sophie hardly heard as her brain tried to process what she was hearing. Her mom's new friend liked to spend a lot of time on the computer and was partial to Cheetos?

Oh, he had to be joking.

Sophie clapped her hands.

"Is everything okay?" Her mom looked at her oddly. "Why are you clapping your hands?"

"Oh, er, just getting in the mood for the concert," Sophie improvised as Malik appeared over by her closet and did a little half wave at her mom (who, thankfully, couldn't see it). "And speaking of which, I really need to finish getting ready."

"Of course," her mom said, and walked out of the room. The minute she was gone, Sophie turned to where Malik was standing.

"You? You were MG?"

"Malik the Ghost, at your service." Malik dropped into a deep bow, and then he clicked his fingers. Suddenly

Zac Efron was gone and a woman with dark hair and an overly bright smile was standing in front of her, wearing what looked like one of her mom's old pottery tops. Sophie continued to stare at him.

"But I don't understand. How? And why? And how all over again?

"You made me promise to stop your mom from selling the house, and when the haunting thing didn't work out, I figured I needed to do something I was more suited to." Malik shrugged, his voice still sounding totally the same, despite the fact he was now a woman.

"Since when have you been suited to talking to my mom on the Internet?" Sophie continued to stare at him in...well, actually, there were no words for what she was feeling. Though *"ewh"* would probably come close.

"Hey, I'll have you know that I'm a very sociable fellow. And I actually tried to tell you I was making progress on it the other day, but then you were too busy trying to decide whether to take the turquoise pill."

"But that's just so...wrong." Sophie shuddered.

"Why? Your mom's a nice lady. In fact, she's a very nice lady. I like her a lot, so trust me, it wasn't hard to talk to her. And by the way, you know you should really try to stop acting so secretive because she really worries about that."

"What, you mean like I should just pretend that I'm not a djinn and that my ghostly djinn guide isn't sitting up on my computer chatting up my mom?"

"Exactly," Malik agreed in a happy voice before he started to frown. "But don't worry. Now that I know your dad is Tariq the Awesome, I will step aside."

"Step aside?" Sophie widened her eyes. Could this conversation get any grosser? Wait, don't answer that.

"That's right." Malik nodded as he smoothed down his T-shirt. Then he clicked his fingers, and he was Zac Efron again. "You've got nothing to worry about. Besides, I'm probably too young for her anyway."

Sophie's eyes widened some more. "Malik, you might look like Zac on the outside, but on the inside, you're two thousand years old. My mom's thirty-seven. Then there is the fact that she thinks you're *a woman*."

"Hey, she's just had four years of grieving. I didn't want to scare her off," Malik protested. "But there was a connection there. I could feel it. And didn't you think that her eyes lit up ever so slightly whenever she mentioned my name?"

"And let's not forget that you're a ghost as well." Sophie ignored his question due to the fact that the whole conversation was just wrong.

"There's no reason to get snippety." Malik poked his chin into the air and sniffed. "Besides, I think you're missing the fact that I managed to stop her from selling the house."

"You did," Sophie was forced to concede as she tried to stop herself from mentally shuddering. *But ewh.* She took another moment and tried to find the positive angle.

"And I suppose the important thing to remember is that you helped her get her pottery mojo back, so thank you for that. I really appreciate it."

"Oh, it's nothing." Malik waved off her thanks. "I just happened to read somewhere in Rufus's book that you should always try to make your djinn student's life as uncomplicated as possible, and this one seemed like an easy fix."

"Well, I am really grateful. I thought I was Montana bound for sure."

"Again, it's my pleasure. And you know, it's not that I wish Tariq ill, but if we happen to find out that he's—"

"No." Sophie shook her head.

"But you don't know what I was going to say," Malik protested.

"True, but there is nothing you can say to make me think my mom would date a two-thousand-year-old djinn ghost," Sophie assured him. "Besides, I'm going to find my dad and bring him home to us."

"Okay, well, you can't blame me for trying." Malik gave a shrug of his shoulders. "And speaking of which, it's been a very trying day, so would you mind zapping me up some Cheetos before you go to that concert of yours?"

For a moment Sophie just stared at him before she heard a car pull up outside. She darted to the window and saw that it was Jonathan Tait and his brother. Harvey and Kara were already in the back. Sophie immediately grabbed her jacket and her bag, pausing only to check that her ticket was still in there. Then she turned to Malik, conjured up three bags of Cheetos and a tube of Pringles (just to mix it up), and then raced down the stairs to try to reach the front door before her mom got there. On the way down, Mr. Jaws hissed at her before Meg told him to shut up because it was the part where the great white attacked a whale.

Sophie grinned as she opened the door. Okay, so her life hadn't turned out quite the way she'd planned (especially the part where her ghostly djinn guide was crushing on her mom), but thankfully she was a positive thinker, which meant as far as she could tell, life was still pretty good.

Turn the page for a peek at the next book…

Sophie's MIXED-UP Magic

Under a Spell

THERE WERE MANY THINGS THAT SOPHIE CAMPBELL was good at; unfortunately, basketball wasn't one of them. In fact, as far as she was concerned, instead of making basketball part of PE, it should be banned on the grounds that it was humiliating and cruel to short people like herself. She had also apparently been at the back of the line when hand-eye coordination was being passed out, which made it even worse. It wasn't like she wasn't a positive person, because she was. A really, really positive person. But seriously, how could anyone be positive when she was surrounded by other people's armpits?

Sophie's two best friends, Kara and Harvey, looked equally unimpressed as they all sat in the bleachers of Robert Robertson Middle School's gym on Monday afternoon, waiting for the ritual humiliation to begin. It was worst for Harvey, who was tall and skinny and looked like he should be able to play. Unfortunately, he tended to think of the ball as a weapon of mass destruction that should be avoided at all costs, which didn't exactly lend itself to success in the sport.

At that moment their PE teacher, Miss Carson, realized that the three of them were still sitting, and she waved for them to come down onto the court.

"And I mean now, Harvey Trenton," the teacher added when Harvey shot her a blank look. He reluctantly untangled his lanky legs, blew his bangs out of his eyes, and jogged over. Sophie and Kara trailed unenthusiastically behind him and joined the rest of the class doing warm-up lunges. Still, not even the prospect of playing basketball could ruin Sophie's mood. Especially when so many great things had happened to her since she had entered sixth grade just over three weeks ago.

For a start, she and her friends were all in the same homeroom (score). Then there was the fact that over the weekend they had managed to get backstage at the Neanderthal Joe concert, where Eddie Henry (the best bass player In. The. World) had given Sophie his guitar pick. And finally, the icing on top of Sophie's deliciously gorgeous pink cupcake was that she and Jonathan Tait had shared "a moment."

It had been just after Eddie had given her the guitar pick. In her excitement Sophie had spilled the contents of her purse, and Jonathan had immediately dropped to the ground to help her gather everything up. *And that's when it happened.* They had both reached for her camera at the same time, causing their fingers to touch. Sophie immediately felt a jolt of electricity go zooming through her, and, as their eyes locked, she tightened her grasp on Jonathan's fingers. It was perfect (and she didn't care what Harvey said, because she knew a moment when she had one, and this most definitely was one).

She let out a dreamy sigh as her fingers tightened around the guitar pick, which was now hanging from her neck on a delicate silver chain. Like she said, a lot had happened in the last few weeks, and—

"Soph, watch out," Kara's voice suddenly cut into her thoughts. Sophie looked up just in time to see a basketball heading straight for her nose.

She instinctively went to lift her hands to stop it from hitting her, but her fingers were tangled in the chain around her neck. There was no way she wanted to break it, but she didn't want to break her face either, which meant there was only one other thing she could do.

She closed her eyes and wished for the ball not to hit her.

A nanosecond later a telltale tingle went racing through her body like a sugar rush, and she saw the ball come to a halt, just inches from her face. It hovered there for what seemed like ten hours before it dropped harmlessly down at her feet.

Oh, she should probably also mention the other thing that had happened since she'd started sixth grade: she had kind of become a djinn.

That's right, a djinn. As in a genie, complete with

magic, orange skin, and immortality. She even had her own ghostly djinn guide called Malik, who was supposed to be showing her the ropes but instead spent most of his time eating Cheetos, downloading stuff from the Internet, and annoying Sophie on a regular basis. And for some weird reason, despite the fact he could shape-shift into anyone he wanted, he had taken to looking like Zac Efron, right down to the streaky caramel-colored hair and navy blue eyes.

At first Sophie had been tempted to take a special reversal pill so that her life could go back to normal. But then she discovered that her dad, who had walked out four years ago, was actually a djinn, too. And so she had kept her powers so that she would be allowed to see the Djinn Council and ask for its help in finding him. Plus, she had to admit that once she'd managed to make her skin look a normal color, being a djinn definitely had its uses. Like stopping flying basketballs and helping her get backstage passes to meet Neanderthal Joe.